The MISADVENTURES of NICHOLAS NABB

The Misadventures of Nicholas Nabb
An original concept by author Jenny Moore
© Jenny Moore

Cover artwork by Marco Guadalupi

Published by MAVERICK ARTS PUBLISHING LTD
Studio 11, City Business Centre, 6 Brighton Road,
Horsham, West Sussex, RH13 5BB
+44 (0) 1403 256941
© Maverick Arts Publishing Limited May 2021

A CIP catalogue record for this book is available
at the British Library.

ISBN: 978-1-84886-775-8

The MISADVENTURES of NICHOLAS NABB

JENNY MOORE

To Dafydd, Lucy and Daniel...
to all the adventures we've shared,
with many more to come

Black Widow

"Good heavens, what's that dreadful smell?" cried the posh old fart in the top hat. His bristled 'tache twitched like a dog's tail as the stink hit his nostrils. My stink. When you've lived down the sewers as long as I have, you don't really notice the pong anymore. Everyone else does, though.

Top Hat adjusted his eyeglass and peered down at me, just as the bread roll disappeared into my pocket.

"Why, you little crook! You thieving guttersnipe!"

Curses! Here we go again. I ducked down under his legs and tore out of the baker's shop, taking my stink and my roll with me.

"After him!" A flurry of outraged cries followed me out onto the street. "Don't let him get away!"

"Stop! Thief!" Anyone would think I was making off with the crown jewels.

"Come back here you little wretch!"

I don't think so, mister.

The chase was on. Top Hat himself was no trouble at all—I managed to ditch him before we reached Mallerton Lane, but the baker's boy who flew out the shop after us was a whole different basket of buns. For a big pudding of a fellow, with a fat wobbly head like an over-risen ball of dough, he was surprisingly quick on his feet. And given that I hadn't eaten anything but gutter-scraps for the best part of a week, mine wasn't the speediest of getaways. Hollow legs can only carry you so far. Halfway across Bartfield Square he caught me, good and proper; snared me like a fish on the end of his flour-fingered line. There was the stolen bread roll, peeping out of my pocket at the gathering crowds. And there *I* was, twisting and jerking round like an eel, struggling to get free.

Floured hands tightened round my collar.

"You're not going anywhere, you thieving little rat," hissed the baker's boy, his yeasty breath hot and damp against my face. "Caught you red-handed." He thrust his knee towards my bulging pocket, forcing the roll up and out from its hiding place. It dropped to the ground, and was set upon by a mangy-looking dog with foaming spit strings hanging from its jaws.

The crowd gasped and cheered like we were part of a Punch & Judy show put on for their entertainment.

"That's the way to do it!"

"Teach the thieving little beggar a lesson!"

"Send for the police," bellowed a big beardy man. "Lock him up and throw away the key!"

"They're on their way," someone shouted back.

Gulp. I was a goner and I knew it. Everyone knew it.

Only that's when the lady in the black veil appeared. One minute there was just a sea of jeering people all round me, and the next minute there she was. Like a grieving angel. I couldn't see her face—not with the thick crêpe hanging down from her widow's mourning bonnet—but she had long shiny angel hair, spilling out across her shoulders, and her voice was soft and low, like velvet.

"There you are, Nicholas," she said, stopping right

in front of me. "Why on earth did you run off like that?"

"What...? Me...? I don't..." I stood there staring at her, my mouth hanging open. How did she know my name?

The baker's boy looked surprised too. His doughy chins quivered as he turned from the lady to me and back again.

"You mean you *know* him?" he stammered at last, as if to say, *what's a nice young widow like you doing with a stinking gutter thief like him?* "But he's a roll-pincher, ma'am."

"Of course I know him," she said. "Master Nabb and I are old friends, aren't we? I sent him on ahead to fetch me a roll while I was talking to the vicar. Only I must have forgotten to give you the money, Nicholas," she added, laying a black-gloved hand on my filthy arm. "How silly of me. And how silly of you to run off without explaining. No wonder this gentleman imagined you were stealing from him."

"But he was spotted, stuffing it into his pocket when he thought no one was looking," argued the baker's boy, turning red and puffing out his chest at the use of the word 'gentleman'.

"That's because I asked him to keep it warm for me, didn't I, Nicholas?" The lady sniffed the air, like she was breathing in fresh oven-baked rolls, instead of stale sewer-stink. "I do so love the smell of warm bread."

"Huh," I grunted, too shocked and confused to manage proper words. Where had she sprung from, and why was she lying for me? It wasn't a very good lie, admittedly—there were more holes in her story than my trousers, and that was saying something. What sort of angel lady wants grubby sewer-hands all over her luncheon bread? Let alone the dubious contents of *my* rat-bitten pockets... But it was nice of her to try, whoever she was. And, amazingly, the baker's boy seemed to be lapping it all up as if he actually believed her. P'rhaps it was the formal widow's weeds that swung it for him. As if a poor grieving woman like her *had* to be telling the truth.

"Sorry, miss," he said, releasing me from his iron grip and straightening up my shirt collar. "My mistake. Don't worry, I'll explain everything to the coppers when they get here. Tell them it was all a misunderstanding."

"The police?" said the lady, with a sharp intake of breath. "Surely we don't need to drag *them* into this? The poor boy's been through quite enough already." I couldn't have agreed more. If I was lucky, they'd bang me up in a cell with a bunch of hardened thieves and murderers. If I wasn't, they'd send me back to the orphanage. To Mr Rodfear and his horrible stick.

The lady fumbled in her purse as the first shrill blasts of a police whistle sounded in the distance. "Please," she told the baker's boy, thrusting a handful of coins at him. "Take this for the inconvenience and let's say no more about it. Come on, Nicholas," she added, slipping her arm through mine and tugging me away. She was surprisingly strong for an angel. "Let's get you home before you cause any more trouble."

"Home?" I said, as she pulled me down a small side street, out of sight of the crowds. "You mean the sewers?" A rare flush of shame spread across my cheeks at the thought of a fine lady like her knowing where I lived. As if she hadn't already guessed by the state of me. Her nose must've been twitching the whole time. "But we're going the wrong way, miss. *My* tunnel's back that way."

Another sharp whistle sounded behind us. It was closer this time. Much closer.

"Hurry," she said, breaking into an undignified trot, the black fabric of her skirts billowing out behind her. "I know somewhere safe we can go." She twisted her head sideways as we ran, like she was examining me. I imagined dark eyes weighing me up from behind their gloomy veiled curtain. "You do like pies, don't you?"

Well now. There were much more important questions that needed answering—I knew that. Like, *who are you exactly? How come you know my name? Why are you helping me? What happened to your husband?* But now probably wasn't the time to ask. Not with the coppers hot on our heels. I put them out of my mind as best as I could and concentrated on *her* question instead:

You do like pies, don't you?

As Nice As Pie

P'rhaps skipping off after a black-veiled stranger on the promise of hot pastry was asking for trouble. But offers like that don't come round too often. Never, in fact. And she *had* just saved my neck. Besides, I was that hungry I'd have followed Spring-Heeled Jack himself for a bite of beef and gravy.

"Why are you doing this?" I asked, as we stood, breathless, inside Mrs Grubson's Pastry Pie Emporium. It was a grand name for such a small shop, but the meaty scent drifting out from the ovens was pure heaven. You might not notice the bad smells after a few months in the sewers, but it makes the good ones better than ever. "I mean, I'm grateful and all that, but I don't really understand." No one else had shown me any kindness in the long months since my escape from the orphanage. No one ever put their nice clean arm round me, or acted like I was something more than muck on the bottom of their shoe. "And how come you know who I am?" That was the bit that *really* got me. I mean, even Mr Rodfear never called me by my real name. I was always just 'lazy good-for-nothing boy' or 'ungrateful little wretch'. Like I should be thanking him for the chance to unpick old rope 'til my fingers bled, and for beating me senseless every night. "Have we met before?" I tried sneaking a sideways glance at her face, past the thick edge of her veil.

She flinched, jerking her head away. "Not now. I'll explain everything soon, I promise. But not here. Not like this."

I nodded, pretending I understood. But really I was more confused than ever. Who *was* she? And what did she mean by *everything*?

"So," she said, changing the subject. "What would you like, Nick? Do you mind if I call you that?"

I shrugged. "'Course not." It was kind of nice to have a proper name again. Better than 'thieving ruffian' or 'smelly urchin'. Besides, I'd answer to anything under the sun if it came with one of Mrs Grubson's delicious-smelling pies. Whoever my mystery angel was, she knew the way to a boy's heart, alright. Or his stomach, which was pretty much the same thing.

"What would you like then, Nick? Beef, mutton, kidney or eel?"

"I er..." That was a trickier one. After months of trampled leftovers and stolen scraps, I'd have sold my own toes for a bit of pie crust and hot air. How was I s'posed to choose when they all sounded as delicious as each other?

"Or how about one of each?" she suggested.

One of each! Blimey. P'rhaps she really *was* an angel.

"Will you be able to manage that many, do you think?"

Could I manage four steaming helpings of pastry heaven? Is rain wet? Does the Queen pee in a silver potty?

Actual speech seemed to have deserted me all of a sudden, so I settled for a simple nod, my belly gurgling a special reply of its own.

"Good. Because you clearly need feeding up a bit," she said, ruffling my sewage-matted hair in a motherly fashion. Least I imagined that was the sort of thing mothers did. Back when I used to dream about *my* mum, she was always running her fingers through my hair, and telling me how she hadn't wanted to leave me. How she'd never leave me again. Only Mr Rodfear said it was my dad who handed me over to the orphanage. And *he* never came back for me neither.

"Feeding up. Feeding up." I repeated it under my breath like a prayer. Apart from 'pies' and 'one of each', I don't think I'd ever heard more beautiful-sounding words than those.

"I'll take a beef, a mutton, an eel and a kidney please, Mrs Grubson," she told the round, red-faced pie-woman, getting some more money out of her purse. An old newspaper cutting slipped out of her pocket at the same time and I scrabbled on the floor to pick it up.

"Coming right up, Annie love," said Mrs Grubson. "Must be extra hungry today!" Then she caught sight of me over the top of the counter as I stood up again, and let out a loud gasp. And she wasn't the only one gasping either, 'cause I'd just clocked what was on that scrap of newspaper. Or rather *who* was on it: 'Missing Boy Steals Orphanage Charity Collection' it said, in big black letters. And there, underneath, was a drawing of me, together with my name: Nicholas Nabb. That solved one mystery at any rate—how a complete stranger seemed to know who I was—but it didn't explain why she was helping me. In fact her kindness made even *less* sense now.

"Gracious me," said Mrs Grubson. "Is that him?"

Annie—my veiled angel—nodded.

No, I thought, still trying to get my head round what I'd seen. They had it all wrong. I mean it *was* me in the paper, even I could see that. But I never took anything from the orphanage when I left. Getting away from Mr Rodfear was all that mattered. Plenty of things had found their way into my pockets *since* then, but not charity money. Never that.

Mrs Grubson was beaming now, like I was the best thing she'd ever clapped eyes on. "You finally found each other then? Oh, congratulations, my love."

Congratulations? Congratulations for what? Tracking down a wanted criminal? And what did she mean, 'finally found each other'? *I* hadn't been looking for anyone.

"Put your money away, love, these are on the house," said Mrs Grubson, still beaming. "After all, it's not every day you—" She stopped short, the smile withering on her lips. "Uh-oh. Coppers coming this way, by the looks of it. You might want to slip out the back while the going's good."

Annie started shaking. I could feel her trembling through the black drapes of her dress. Anyone'd think it was her who'd been pocketing bread rolls. That *she'd* been falsely accused of stealing from innocent orphans. I slipped the newspaper cutting into my pocket before anyone else saw it and got ready to run. As soon as I'd had my pies, that was.

"Thank you," Annie told Mrs Grubson. "Hurry, Nick. This way."

"Wait, what about the pies?" I couldn't leave them now. Not when they were close enough to taste...

"Here, my love," said Mrs Grubson, thrusting them into my waiting arms. "Good luck to the pair of you. Come and see me again when the dust has settled. Let me know you're alright."

"Thank you," said Annie again, dragging me past the hot ovens as they belched out another cloud of steaming meat and eel. "Thank you for everything." And then we were squeezing our way down a narrow, cluttered corridor, past wooden crates and empty barrels, out into a dark, squalid alley running along the back of the shop.

"I didn't do it, you know," I told her, through a mouthful of hot mutton. The taste was every bit as wonderful as the smell. Even better in fact. "I never stole any money from the orphanage, I swear." Mr Rodfear probably took it himself, drinking away the proceeds of his own charity box and then pinning the blame on me. He'd have merrily thrashed me for it too if the police had caught me. Mind, he'd beat a boy just for breathing.

"It wouldn't matter to me if you had," said Annie. We were skirting low along the alley wall like hunted animals. "But it must have been bad in there for you to run away like that."

"Yes, it was." I thought about Mr Rodfear's horrible blackened teeth, and the way he sucked the spit back in round his gums as he raised his hand ready to strike. That stick was his answer to everything. Someone stumbling over his reading lesson? Why, beat him, of course. Working too slowly? Beat him some more. Crying in the middle of the night? Thrash him soundly 'til he stops.

"I'm sorry," said Annie, like it was *her* fault he was such a violent pig of a man. "Quickly. Let's see if we can lose them down here." We took a sharp left at the end of the alley and plunged into a crowded maze of cobbled streets and muck-strewn lanes. It wasn't the easiest of things, running and talking and wolfing down four whole pies, all at the same time, but I gave it my best shot. I managed three of them, anyway. I handed the fourth one to a skinny little thing begging outside a pawnbroker's—she looked like she needed it more than me.

"D'you reckon we're safe now?" I asked, as we stumbled to a panting halt outside a ramshackle theatre. I licked the last few drops of gravy off my lips and stood on tiptoe, trying to see through the throng of scruffy boys who were pushing and shoving to get into the show. "No sign of blue hats. And I can't hear any whistles."

"I... hope... so," Annie wheezed, fighting for air. "I'm not sure I can run any further... My chest..."

She sounded like she was about to keel over, the breath catching in her lungs with an alarming rasping noise.

"Look," I said, pointing to the sign outside the theatre: *Charity Magic Show for Lost Ladies and Homeless Boys.* How perfect was that? "Why don't we hide in there 'til you're feeling better? It'll be nice and dark so no one'll be able to see us." Normally I'd just lay low in the sewers 'til the heat was off again. But I could hardly suggest that to her. "Come on." I brushed off the worst of the pie crumbs and muck, and gave her my arm to lean on. "I don't want you collapsing after everything you've done for me."

"You're a good boy, Nick. I knew you would be."

Me? Good? She didn't know me very well then did she? Then again, I didn't have the first clue who she really was either. Annie Someone-or-other. Grieving widow. Pie angel. It wasn't much to go on.

"You still haven't told me why you're doing this," I said, as we joined the end of the jostling queue. "You saw the newspaper cutting. Why didn't you turn me into the police when you had the chance?"

"Oh Nick," Annie said, twisting round to stroke my hair again. "I'd never do that. No matter what you'd done." And then her hand dropped back down to her side. "Besides, you're not the only one the police are looking for."

"Who? *You?*" Was the widow outfit some kind of cunning disguise? Did she have secret bundles of loot strapped into her skirts?

"I didn't mean to do it." We'd reached the theatre lobby now, and her voice was hushed and urgent. "You have to believe me, Nick. I couldn't bear it otherwise."

"Why? What did you do?" It couldn't be any worse than stealing charity money from orphans. Could it?

"I killed him," she whispered, as the battered theatre door swung shut behind us with a clunk. "I killed my husband."

Abracadabra!

What was I doing, shutting myself up in the murky gloom with a killer? Why didn't I turn straight round and run, while I still had the chance? It's a good question. I mean, anything could've happened, tucked away in the back seats, and no one would've seen until it was too late.

But I couldn't do it. Even while my brain was shouting at my legs to scram—*quick, you fool, before she gets you too*—my heart was telling me to stay. To trust her. It was something about her voice... about the way her fingers felt when she stroked my hair. I still didn't have a clue who she was, or why she'd been looking for me, but there was this strange connection between us. It's hard to explain... like a warm feeling inside. And I don't mean the hot meat and pastry sitting in my stomach. There was a warm glow in my chest as well, every time she said my name. No. I couldn't just leave her, at least not before finding out the truth.

"Why don't you tell me what happened?" I whispered, as a big velvet curtain at the front of the hall began rising up into the air, all on its own. I'd never been to a theatre before. Was that normal or was that part of the magic?

"There was a fire..." Annie began, but her words were drowned out by a sudden burst of clapping and cheering. Judging by the wild whoops and high-pitched shouts there were a whole lot more homeless boys in the audience than there were lost ladies.

"...and then I ran," she finished as the applause died down. "All I knew was I had to get away from there, Nick. I had to find you..."

"Sshhh," hissed a boy to her left, turning round in his seat to glare at us. He was pretty smart-looking from the neck up, with a clean cap and peachy pink cheeks, but his oversized tattered coat would've been right at home in the sewers with me. "I can't hear what he's saying."

The 'he' in question was a tall, green-faced magician with slicked-back hair, who'd appeared on the stage in a swirling plume of smoke. He didn't seem to be saying anything much as far as I could tell—at least not with his voice. It was his hands that were doing all the talking. They pulled a silk snot-rag from his breast pocket and waved it to one side with a flourish. Ta da! There was a funny cooing sound and then the hanky grew wings, fluttering off to the back of the stage, looking for all the world like a white pigeon.

Blimey, I thought, forgetting all about my Pie Angel of Death and her murdered husband. That wasn't something you saw every day.

"Welcome, ladies and young gentlemen," said the magician, with a low, sweeping bow. "I am Žalias the Great, Grand Master of Mystery and Magic. Prepare to be amazed by my impossible enchantments! Get ready for the most remarkable feats of illusion and conjuring the world has ever seen!"

I slid forwards in my chair to get a better look.

"Behold!" he boomed, as the small, cloth-covered table in front of him lifted itself a full foot in the air and hovered there, on invisible wings. I blinked my eyes, over and over, to check I wasn't dreaming— tables couldn't fly any more than I could—but there it was. And even when the magician walked all the way round it, hands clasped behind his back, it *still* floated. But no sooner had he released it back onto the stage, to another wild chorus of cheers and clapping (with me clapping the hardest of anyone), than he was onto the next bit of magic, pulling handful after handful of paper flowers out of an empty cup, and coughing up live frogs.

Trick followed trick. There were solid rings that passed right through each other, levitating ladies, six boys who vanished away inside a locked cupboard, and another five who disappeared behind a floating curtain. Apart from my own special pie-vanishing magic, I'd never seen anything so good in my whole life. He even blew real flames out of his mouth! I noticed Annie turning away at that bit, like she couldn't bear to watch, but I kept on clapping, harder and harder, 'til my palms felt like they were burning too.

By the time he chopped one of the ladies from the front row in half, I was clapping so hard I thought my hands might fall off altogether. Sawed her clean in two, he did, but she never cried out, not even when the squeaking blade reached her flesh and bone. P'rhaps she'd fainted by then. Or p'rhaps there was something magic on the cloth he draped over her face to help her sleep through the pain. If it was me, I'd have been screaming like a baby, begging for him to let me out. Only when he opened up the box afterwards, to show us her bloody, mangled remains, there was nothing there. *Fried bread and flea bites!* She'd been spirited clean away—top half and bottom—leaving nothing but a pair of empty boots sticking out the foot holes.

"And now," said Žalias, "we come to our final trick: what I like to call 'The Grieving Widow'." Annie stiffened in her seat beside me, as two shadowy figures in black dragged a large wooden coffin onto the stage. "We'll need another couple of volunteers for this," the magician added, his assistant spinning the limelight out over the audience. "Come on now, don't be shy."

The boy on the other side of Annie—the one with the smart cap and frowzy old coat—was already up on his feet, waving wildly. He'd volunteered for every trick so far and still hadn't been picked.

"I'll do it," he called out. His voice was high and sing-song. "Pick me!"

The magician smiled, his teeth glowing yellow-green in the gas lamp glare. "Why yes, young man," he said. "You'll do very nicely. I see you've even brought a ready-made widow with you!"

Everyone laughed, except for Annie, who shrank back further into her seat, shaking her head.

"No," she said, her voice little more than a whisper. "Choose someone else. Please." But the magician was already climbing down off the stage and striding along the aisle to fetch her.

"Let's hear it for our brave young friend and the lovely lady in black," he announced, stirring the audience up in a fresh round of applause.

"Here, Nick, I want you to have this." Annie gave me a brass locket from round her neck, pressing it into my hands with her trembling gloved fingers. "In case anything happens." P'rhaps she was worried she was going to get chopped up and vanished away too.

"Why? What is it?" I turned it over, tracing the delicate engraving. The back was warm to the touch where it'd been resting against her skin.

"It's you," she said. I could feel her eyes boring into me through her thick veil. "When you were little."

"What?" I found the clasp at the side of the locket and opened it up. "What do you mean?" There was a tiny curl of hair in one half—brown, like mine—and a faded photograph of a baby in the other. Questions exploded in my head, tumbling over each other in a tangle of happiness and confusion. "Where did you get this? Did my dad give it to you?"

Annie shook her head, like she wanted me to be quiet, but I couldn't keep the words in even if I tried.

"Are those his hands holding me up?" When I looked closely I could see two lots of hairy fingers clasped beneath the baby's arms. "Is he still alive?" Maybe that was what Mrs Grubson had been talking about at the pie shop. *You finally found each other then.* Maybe my dad was still out there and he'd sent Annie to look for me! That *had* to be it. *Oh, please let that be it.* "Where is he?" I asked. "Can you take me to him?"

But Annie didn't answer. Žalias was waiting at the end of the row now, holding out his hand for her and the boy in the coat to join him.

"Come on, ma'am," he coaxed. "No need to be shy. We're all friends here."

Still Annie didn't move.

"Look, she doesn't want to do it," I said. *I* didn't want her to do it either. I wanted her to stay here and tell me everything. "You'll have to find someone else instead." I was about to add how she was still grieving, and it was improper of the magician to even suggest she took part in such a thing. And then I realised it was pretty improper of her to be at a magic show in the first place.

"But you're already dressed for the part," said Žalias, ignoring me completely.

"Oh, alright," Annie eventually agreed, getting to her feet. Her heavy widow skirts brushed against my legs as she shuffled past me. "It doesn't look like I've got any choice in the matter." P'rhaps she figured she'd draw more attention to herself by refusing, than just getting the thing over and done with. "As long as I can keep my veil on," she added. "I don't want anyone to see me. I shouldn't even *be* here."

I clutched her locket tightly inside my fist as if I could squeeze the answers out of it. Why was she so secretive about her looks? Was the thick widow's veil a clever way to hide from the police, or did she have something wrong with her? I tried picturing her face underneath all that black crêpe—horribly disfigured by smallpox scars maybe, or skin all burned away in the fire she was trying to tell me about—but all I saw was a beautiful angel.

"Of course, my dear," said Žalias. "As far as everyone outside these four walls is concerned, you were never here."

The boy followed her out into the aisle, apologising as he squeezed past. "Excuse me," he said, sounding surprisingly posh and proper. Surprisingly polite. "Sorry about this." There was a strange floral smell about him too, lurking under the stale sweat and dirt of his coat, as if he'd been rolling in something sweet and flowery... lavender. Yes, that was it! Like the little perfumed bags the flower girls sold outside the railway station. Wherever he'd come from, it certainly wasn't the sewers.

"Where would you like me to go, sir?" asked the boy, bounding up the wooden steps onto the stage. "I mean, where d'you want me?" His voice switched suddenly from posh and sing-song to common-as-muck, like he couldn't make up his mind which one he was. In fact all of him seemed pretty mixed up when I came to think about it. He was wearing boots, for one thing (not like the other bare-footed boys I'd seen outside earlier), and what looked like dark blue stockings, peeking out from under his coat. He pointed to the velvet-lined coffin. "Shall I get in?"

"No," said Žalias, still smiling. "You are to play the part of the avenging ghost—the poor murdered husband. That coffin's not for you."

Vanishing Act

No wonder Žalias had saved this trick 'til last. It had a bit of everything—smoke, fire and flying—with plenty more besides. One minute the boy was there, and then a curtain came down in front of him and he seemed to be floating above the stage, all wispy and see-through, to a chorus of unearthly moans. He pointed his finger at Annie and *whummmp*, she fell backwards like she'd been struck. Žalias lifted her into the waiting coffin and shut the lid down tight.

"Aaaaarrrrgggghhhhh!"

A piercing scream had us jumping in our seats, then a ring of blue fire came bursting up round the edges of the coffin. I thought about Annie, trapped inside in the darkness, and squeezed the locket even tighter into the palm of my hand. I'd seen how she shrank away from the sight of flames earlier in the show, and now they were all around her. Could she hear them, crackling and spitting as she lay there?

"That's enough!" I called. "Let her out." But even as I was shouting it the flames gave one last upwards flare and died altogether. The ghost of the boy disappeared with them, and Žalias stepped forwards to remove the lid of the coffin. I waited for Annie to sit up—to climb back out—but nothing happened. Žalias levered the heavy base into an upright position and my pies did a full somersault inside my stomach. Annie was gone, leaving nothing but a faint swirl of smoke.

"Thank you, thank you, you're too kind," said the magician, bowing deeply as the audience burst into applause. "Please leave the theatre in an orderly fashion. And if you'd like to see more, come back at the same time tomorrow. Bring all your lost and homeless friends."

"Wait," I yelled. "Where've they gone? Where's Annie?" But the curtain at the front of the stage was already coming down, taking the magician with it.

"Where are they?" I asked again, pulling at the tattered shirtsleeve of a boy in the next row. Something wasn't right. Not one of the vanished boys or ladies had come back, I realised, with another sickening jolt in my stomach.

"Dunno," answered the boy. "Magic, ain't it?"

"No such thing as magic," said his pale-faced neighbour, with a sniff. "It's all done with mirrors and trap doors. I'd try the stage door round the back of the theatre if I was you. And if you see the lads from the locked cupboard trick, tell them we're heading back to the market in search of fresh pickings."

I took his advice, but there was no sign of Annie or the cupboard boys outside the stage door either. No sign of anyone, come to that, just a pair of carriages clattering off up the cobbles towards the bend in the road. My chest tightened as I watched them disappear—what if Annie was on board? What if she'd gone without me?

No, I told myself firmly. She wouldn't have done that. Not when she'd gone to all that trouble to find me in the first place. 'Course not. I tucked the locket into my trouser pocket for safe-keeping and hammered on the door.

Nothing happened. I knocked again and again, harder and harder, 'til my knuckles were red raw, my eyes smarting with the unfairness of it all. But still no one came. Not the magician. Not the vanishing boys. And not Annie. How could she disappear without telling me who she was? Who *I* was? Panicking, I raced round to the front of the theatre, to find the main door all shut up and locked as well. There was a young woman from the audience stood under the portico, waiting for her own missing friend, but she gave it up as a bad job not long after I arrived, deciding she must have gone without her.

What now?

I retraced my steps and hammered on the stage door one last time. "Annie! *Please!* It's me, Nicholas! Nick."

And that's when I heard it. The faintest of cries coming from somewhere down by my feet. From a hidden basement window. "Help!"

"Annie? Is that you?" I flopped down onto the

cobbles beside a still-fresh pile of horse dung, and peered in through the glass. It was so filthy and encrusted with dirt, I hadn't even noticed it before. But when I rubbed at it with my torn cuff I could see something moving on the other side.

"Help! Let us out of here!" came a new cry. It was too high-pitched to be Annie, but they sounded desperate, whoever they were. "Hurry! Before it's too late!"

"Alright," I promised, with more confidence than I felt. The glass looked pretty thick. "Stand back from the window," I ordered, fetching my trusty rat-scarer out of my other pocket. It was a round, heavy stone, with a good straight aim, and had seen off some real monsters in its time. You might get used to the stink of the sewers after a while, but you never get used to the rats; to the clawing scuttle of fur and teeth over your legs when you're trying to sleep. If you haven't got a knife to protect yourself down there, you'd better get yourself a good stone, quick, and learn how to throw it.

Thud! Doof! The scarer bounced clean off the first

couple of tries. But there was a dull splintering sound on the third go and the stone disappeared from view, the glass cracking outwards like a frosted spider's web. I took one last look along the street to check the coast was clear (I'd need more than a mystery pie angel to keep me from the clink if I got done for breaking and entering) and rammed my knee in, hard. Spiky shards showered down from the window to be swallowed up by the darkness below.

"Hello?" I called down after them. "Who's there?"

"It's Edwin," came a familiar sing-song voice. It was the lad from the grieving widow trick, I was sure of it. "And there's a load of boys down here with me. I managed to cut through our ropes and gags with my brother's penknife but we're still locked in. Please— you've got to get us out of here before they come back."

Who were 'they'? Surely not the magician and his assistants? That wouldn't be a very charitable end to their charity show. I didn't stop to puzzle it out though—I had more important things to think about. "Is Annie there too? The lady in the coffin?" I pushed out the last few scraps of glass and leaned my head and shoulders in through the hole for a better look.

"No," said Edwin. "I've no idea what happened to your friend. I'll help you look for her though, I swear, as soon as I get out of here. Please," he said again. "We have to hurry."

"Alright." I bit back my frustration. My search for answers would have to wait. "What shall I do?" As my eyes adjusted to the gloom I could see a small brick cell of a room, with a line of boys huddled against the wall. "I've tried all the doors out here already," I told Edwin. "They're locked fast."

He thought for a moment. "Can we squeeze through that window, do you think?"

"Probably." I wasn't exactly big for my age, admittedly—you don't tend to grow tall and fat on an orphanage diet—but I was practically halfway through already. "So long as you breathe in and watch out for glass splinters. You'll have to lose the coat though."

"Alright. I'll give the others a leg-up from down here, and you pull them out the other side," said Edwin. "You're first," he told a little blonde boy with sticky-out jug ears. "Up you go now."

Oof. It was hard work, hauling someone up like that, even a little whipster like Jug Ears. I thought my arms were going to tear clean out their sockets. But I wedged my shoulder against the wall, so I didn't tumble back down with him, and tugged like my life depended on it. Which it did really. 'Cause if anyone caught us—the kidnappers themselves, or some rich old fart passer-by—we were *all* for it. I wouldn't see them coming, either, with my eyes screwed shut to keep out the biting sting of sweat and dirt. But at last I heaved him clear of the broken window, with only a tiny bit of blood down his shins and another couple of gashes up my arm.

The next boy was easier 'cause there were two of us on the job. And then three, and four... It wasn't 'til we got to boy number eleven that I realised we had a problem. Who was going to help Edwin up from the bottom when he was the only one left down there?

I scanned the street for something we could use— something small enough to lower down through the window, but big enough for him to stand on. There was nothing though. Just another dollop of dung, a well-chewed mutton bone, and a pile of sodden old rags, which fell apart in my hands when I went to pick them up. They did give me an idea though...

"Here, Edwin," I called down to him. "What about those bits of rope they tied you up with? If you knotted them all together we could pull you up that way."

"Of course!" he shouted back. "You're a genius."

Me? A genius? No one had ever called me that before. Heinous, yes (as in, *what's that heinous smell?*), but never genius. I was still grinning to myself when he shouted, "Catch!"

A snaking length of knotted rope came flying up towards me and I grabbed hold of the end with both hands, wrapping it round my wrist for good measure. One of the other boys—a freckled redhead with a turned-up nose—took hold of it further along and we braced ourselves ready to pull.

"That's it. All set. Up you come."

Cold cuts and cholera! How'd he get so blinking heavy on stolen food and street scraps? The other boys had been hard enough, but Edwin weighed a tonne. And that was without his hefty coat on. Still, I gritted my teeth and got on with it as best as I could. The sooner he was out of there, the sooner we'd all be safe. And the sooner I could get back to looking for Annie.

He must have been a good halfway up the wall to freedom when we heard it: the distant clop of hooves and the clatter of wooden wheels against the cobbles.

Uh-oh.

"There's someone coming! Let's get out of here." The other boys scattered, like lice fleeing from the squish of fingertips, leaving the two of us—me and Freckles—hanging there on the end of the rope: a pair of sitting targets. Or should that be lying-down targets? Either way we were in big trouble.

"Hurry up," I shouted down through the window, the muscles in my arms burning pure fire as I pulled and tugged and strained. "We've got to get out of here. Fast!" The noise from the carriage was louder now.

"You're right," said Freckles. "I'm not going back down there again. You're on your own, I'm afraid." And with that he let go of the rope and did a disappearing trick all of his own.

5

A Bad Case of the Runs

That wasn't good. It wasn't good at all. Edwin was heavy enough before, with two of us hauling him up, but now it felt like an elephant swinging on the other end of the rope. An enormous, lumbering circus elephant, like the ones in the street parades, only without the music and cheering. Just the sound of that carriage getting nearer and nearer. It'd be coming round the bend at any moment and then we'd both be done for.

"Come on! Faster!" I hissed, willing him on, even though I knew it was all down to me now. "We've got company." The rope was cutting so deep into my wrists it's a wonder it didn't slice my hands clean off.

"I think I can see a chink in the wall," came the

muffled reply. "One more tug and I might be able to reach it with my foot."

One more tug. I didn't have any more tug left in me! But I'd never find Annie if I got caught now. I'd never find out the truth about the man in the locket if they shut me up in the basement too. I clenched every muscle in my body—from my fists to my bum cheeks—and pulled. And pulled. I could've done with some magic of my own, right then. A levitation spell, ideally. And a nice bit of smoke to hide us from whoever it was in that carriage.

Abracadabra! Some of the weight seemed to lift, all of a sudden. Edwin must have reached that chink in the wall. And then he was thrusting himself up again as I pulled, and before I knew it he was there, clawing at the window frame with his hands, scrabbling to haul himself through.

It was a tight squeeze—a *very* tight squeeze—but he made it. We threw ourselves into the shadows of a dark doorway as the carriage came clattering round the bend, slowing to a halt outside the stage door.

Two men in top hats clambered down from the cab,

brushing themselves off with their leather-gloved fingers. The taller of the pair—who looked an awful lot like Žalias the Great, only without the grass green skin—reached back up and pressed a small velvet pouch into the driver's hand.

"A little something extra for your continued discretion," he said. "Remember, if anyone asks, you were never here. And you don't know anything about any missing ladies. Got it?"

The driver nodded, stuffing the pouch into his dark overcoat. "Discretion's my middle name, sir. As always. You can count on me."

"That's him," whispered Edwin, pointing to the second Top Hat. "That chap there with the magician. He's the one who locked me up after I fell through the trapdoor." He shuddered at the memory. "One minute I was inside a strange mirrored contraption on stage, with a ghost version of me floating up over my head, and then *whoosh!* Straight down into a waiting sack and bundled into that basement room, ready to be trussed up like a Christmas turkey. They'd probably have had my giblets too if you hadn't got me out of there!"

"Probably," I agreed, like I was an expert on trussing and giblets. And Christmas. The only turkeys I'd ever seen were the unplucked ones strung up outside the butcher's. Wouldn't want to end up like one of them, that's for sure.

"What do you think?" asked Edwin as the carriage clattered away again. "Make a dash for it now, before they spot the broken window, or stay here and hope for the best?"

I didn't answer. I was trying to hear what Žalias and his friend were saying, hoping for a clue about Annie. But the only words I managed to catch were 'fresh delivery', 'fair' and 'freak', and no matter how hard I twisted them round in my brain, they still didn't give me any answers. Part of me wanted to march straight up to the pair of them, demanding to know where she was. But only a little part of me. The stupid, reckless part. The rest of me knew better. I'd be no good to her if I was trussed up in a basement like one of Edwin's turkeys. They'd be after *my* giblets, then, supposing I had any.

"So?" said Edwin, dragging my attention back to more urgent matters of survival. "Run or hide? What do you think?"

In the end, it didn't matter what I thought. We were running, whether I liked it or not.

"What in blue blazes has been going on here?" cried the magician, finally noticing the broken window. "The little rats have escaped! But that's impossible."

"Now!" cried Edwin, grabbing me by the elbow and flinging us out of the doorway, into full view of the two men. "RUN!"

I didn't need telling twice. I scrammed, sprinting down the lane like a dog with a firecracker up its backside. Seemed like I'd spent half the day running but at least I had proper food in my belly this time, helping me on. Powered by pies, that was me.

"Look!" came an angry cry from behind. The magician again by the sounds of it. "There's two of the little wretches there! Don't let them get away."

He was wrong, of course. There only one runaway wretch, and one window-smashing accomplice, but I wasn't about to stop and explain.

I could already hear them pelting along the cobbles after us.

My mind was racing almost as fast as my legs as we flew past a row of fair posters pasted across a pub wall. A fair on Blackthorn Common... could that be what the magician meant? *Fresh delivery... Fair... Freak...* The words pounded round my head in time with my feet as we doubled back down the next street and zigzagged across a crowded square of market stalls. Had Žalias sold Annie and the others to a fairground freak show, to be covered in feathers and trundled out as a new flock of bird ladies?

"Quick, down here," called Edwin, pointing to a hidden alley, strewn with crumpled sheets of newsprint and mounds of old vegetable peelings. I skidded and scrambled along after him, gashing my elbow open on a bit of jutting-out metal as I ran. But there was no time to worry about the blood trickling down my arm. I forced myself on, faster and faster.

"Stop right there!" came a shout from behind, closely followed by a thump—the dull thud of a heavy body hitting the ground—and curses far too colourful to repeat. My heart gave a small lurch of triumph. One down, one to go.

And then Žalias was shouting too, but not at us: "Stop groaning and get up! I don't give two hoots about your twisted ankle. We can't let them get away. If they go to the police we're done for."

Me? Go to the police? Not likely.

"Turn right at the end and head for the river," I yelled at Edwin, like he was a hundred yards ahead of me instead of a couple of paces. But as soon as we turned out into the busy shopping street at the end, I yanked him back and we barrelled off to the left instead. If we could just throw them off our scent long enough to get away or hide...

Hang on a minute, what was that? Yes! A sewer hatch, or 'one of my back doors' as I liked to think of them. Home, sweet home. Alright, maybe not the sweet bit, but so much the better. Nothing throws people off your scent like escaping down a stinky sewer. And toffs hate getting cack-water in their shoes, so they never come looking for you.

I was a dab hand at prising entrance covers off in a

hurry, but this one was proving tricky. "Here, give me a hand with this," I told Edwin. "We've got ourselves a stiff one here."

He looked at me like I was off my nut. "But... but... we can't go down there. It's a sewer!"

"True," I agreed, working round the edges with my fingers, "but it's home. Trust me. We'll be quite safe."

"You mean you actually *live* down there?" Now he was looking at me like I'd escaped naked from Bedlam with my pants on my head. "But isn't it full of...?"

"'Course it is. Hundreds and thousands of them, I should think, bobbing around like smelly little boats on a great big river of piddle. Only you can't see them in the dark." I couldn't help laughing at the expression on his face as he drank it all in (my words, that is, not the sludgy piddle river). He was a different breed of homeless boy to the usual crowd, that's for sure. That's if he *was* homeless, what with that posh voice he kept slipping in and out of, and his lavender smell and fancy stockings. In fact, apart from the rips where he'd caught himself on the broken basement window, his whole outfit looked pretty fine and fancy without the ratty overcoat. Even his fingernails were clean! But now wasn't the time to puzzle it all out. It was just one more mystery to add to all the other strange events of the day. And to be fair to him, posh pretender or not, he got down on his knees all the same and helped me tug the cover loose.

"After you," I said, gesturing down the ladder into the darkness. "And don't worry about the turds," I added, helpfully, as he gagged on the rising gases. "They don't bite. They leave that to the rats."

Laying Low

"See," I panted, as we perched together on a dry-ish curve of brick tunnel. Not that we could see much down there in the dark. "It's not so bad really."

"As long as you don't breathe in," said Edwin. "You *really* live down here?"

"'Fraid so. This isn't my normal patch, mind. I bunk down in an old access tunnel a bit further north. How about you? Got a particular shop doorway you like to call 'home'?"

"Er… no… not really," said Edwin. "A *sewer* though," he added, turning the conversation back to me. "Imagine that! And there was me thinking the horrible smell at the magic show was coming from my coat!"

The magic show. A fresh rush of anger rose in my chest as I pictured the three of us—me, Edwin and Annie—clapping away at Žalias' tricks, without the first clue what was coming our way. It was my fault Annie was gone. I was the one who suggested we hid out in the theatre. And now she'd vanished, taking the answers to all my questions with her.

Edwin was more interested in his abandoned coat though. "I wouldn't be surprised if it was infested with lice," he said, scratching away in the darkness. "That rag and bottle man saw me coming a mile off, didn't he? *He* should have paid *me* to take it off his hands."

"You'll be cold without it tonight, though," I told him, "lice or no lice."

"No," said Edwin. "I'll be tucked up nice and warm in…" He broke off, realising his mistake. "I mean er… I'll be alright. I'll think of something."

Ha! Gotcha! I *knew* there was something fishy about him. What kind of street urchin wears polished boots and smells of lavender?

"You're not really homeless at all, are you?" I said, swinging my feet against the damp brickwork.

"Not that it matters," I added. "We've all got our little secrets…" Like the newspaper clipping hidden away inside my pocket. The one naming Nicholas Nabb as an orphanage charity box thief. I knew the smart thing to do was get rid of it—float it away on an underground river of sewage where no one'd ever find it—but I couldn't bring myself to do it. Not yet. Not when Annie had carried it round with her all this time. It would've been like throwing away a little bit of her. I still didn't have the first clue who she was, or how she knew me, but there was some kind of bond between us. I'd felt it at the theatre and I could still feel it, even now.

"You're right," Edwin admitted. "I'm not who you think I am. I'm sorry for lying when you've been so good to me, Nick, it's just…" But that was as far as his confession went. "Look, let's not talk about that now," he said. "I want to hear about this Annie of yours. I promised I'd help you find her."

My Annie? Huh! If only. I'd have given anything to belong to someone, 'specially someone who helped me escape from the police and plied me with hot pies.

"Who is she?" asked Edwin. "Where does she live? We should probably try her home address first, in case she managed to get away somehow."

"That's the problem. I don't know who she is or where she comes from. I don't even know if Annie's her real name." I filled him in on the day's strange events, starting with the bread roll sitting there on the tray, calling to me like a long-lost friend. It seemed like a lifetime ago now. "...And then she got called up to do the magic trick with you," I finished, "before I could ask her any more about the photograph in the locket. About my dad."

Edwin gave a low whistle. "Lordy, it's like something out of a novel, isn't it?"

Was it? The only book we ever read at the orphanage was the Bible, which doubled up as a handy thwacker when Mr Rodfear was testing us on our commandments. Thou shalt not steal—thwack! Thou shalt not bear false witness—thwack, thwack! Thou shalt not go looking through Mr Rodfear's private ledgers—thwack, thwack and double thwack. That last one wasn't a proper commandment, but I got a few belts across the side of my head with the Bible all the same when I got caught leafing through the orphanage records in search of the truth about my dad…

There it was, in Mr Rodfear's horrible spidery handwriting. There I was:

Name: Nicholas Nabb

Age on arrival: 2 weeks

Parentage: Unknown. Deposited by unnamed father—refused to supply any family details.

Additional Notes: Robust-looking child, unlike his weak excuse for a father. Cried like a woman when he handed the brat over (along with generous donation towards his upkeep).

That was it. That was all the record there was of my family. But I held on to the mention of my dad's tears; clutching at the idea that he hadn't wanted to give me up—that he'd come back for me when he could—even as Mr Rodfear was pounding at my head with the Bible.

"How dare you sneak into my office and look through my papers, you miserable little snot-face?!" I don't think he'd ever hit me so hard. It was a good fortnight or so before I could hear out of my left ear again.

"You told me my parents were dead," I yelled back between blows. The pain thrumming round my skull felt like it belonged to someone else, and the thought of my dad, still alive out there somewhere, made me more reckless than ever. *"But what about my father? What about the money he left for me?"*

"Dead within the year, I'd have thought," Mr Rodfear jeered, showering me with righteous flecks of saliva. *"No strength or substance to the man. If you could call him a man."* Thwack. *"Barely filled his own britches. First snap of cold weather would have finished him off. And good riddance too."*

"No," I told him, hot tears mixing with the blood trickling from my ear. *"You're wrong. He's not dead. He's coming back for me. I know it."*

Thwack! *"That's enough of your insolence. If I say the man's dead, then he's dead. And you'd better start showing me some respect, unless you want to join him…"*

I did want to join him, more than anything, but in this life, not the next.

It was another couple of years before the last drops of hope ran out, before I gave up waiting and left to make a new life for myself on the streets. Mr Rodfear must've been right all along, I'd realised. Dad really was dead, wasn't he? Because otherwise he'd have come back for me. Only now I wasn't so sure… What if he'd sent Annie to find me?

Edwin had dropped quiet, as if he was thinking. "I'm sorry," he said at last. "If I hadn't volunteered for the grieving widow trick, the magician might have picked someone else instead of Annie. You could be tucked up in some cosy pie shop together even now…"

"The pie shop," I repeated like an echo. But this time my mind was focussed on something more than warm pastry and melt-in-your-mouth meaty chunks of heaven. "That's it!"

"It is?"

"Yes!" Why didn't I think of that before? "As soon as the coast is clear we'll head back to Mrs Grubson's pie shop. I'm pretty sure *she* knows who Annie is. And I've got a funny feeling she knows who I am too."

All the Fun
of the Fair

There was no sign of the magician or his angry sidekick when we emerged, blinking, into the sunshine. We'd lost them. Edwin took a deep breath, like he was drinking in the fresh air, and pulled a flashy watch from his waistcoat pocket.

My eyes nearly popped out their sockets. "Blimey, is that gold?" A watch like that could feed a boy for a whole year.

Edwin nodded. "Yes. I mean, I expect so. It's not really mine of course—I pinched it, didn't I? That's right. I pinched it off some rich old toff outside the theatre."

He was a terrible liar. If he *had* pinched it from someone, it was more likely to be a lady, judging by the ornate flowery pattern round the outside, but I didn't believe him for one minute.

"Look," I said. "It's fine. You don't have to pretend with me." Why he'd want anyone to think he was a homeless ragamuffin was the real puzzler—p'rhaps it was all a ploy to get into the magic show—but it was no skin off my nose. "And you don't have to stay and help me, neither, if you don't want to. If you've got somewhere else you need to be…"

"What? And miss out on solving the mystery of the locket?" Edwin grinned. "No chance. Besides," he added, "I'd still be down in that basement if it wasn't for you. Or worse." He glanced over his shoulder, as if Žalias and his friend might still be lurking, ready to pounce. "Come on, before they come back. To the pie shop!"

"Hello there, my dears," said Mrs Grubson, her face redder and sweatier than ever. "What can I get for…?" She stopped, eyes narrowing in the generous bulge of her cheeks, as she clocked me properly. "Wait a minute, it's you, isn't it? Annie's lad?" The ready smile fell away from her lips. "They didn't catch her, did they? Tell me that's not why you're here."

"*They* didn't," I said. "The coppers, I mean, but I think someone else has taken her."

"Who?"

"A magician. He vanished her away in one of his tricks and she never came back."

"He's bad news," cut in Edwin. "But we don't know anything for sure. We thought you might know where to start looking for her. Whereabouts she'd go if she managed to get away."

"Hang on," I said, playing back the pie-woman's words. A crazy idea had just popped into my head. "You called me 'Annie's lad'." It *was* crazy, wasn't it? I mean, I'd always thought my mum had died in childbirth. That's why Dad handed me over to Mr Rodfear. He couldn't very well care for a newborn on his own, and keep down a steady job.

"Yes," said Mrs Grubson, looking puzzled. "That's right, isn't it? She's been searching for you these last few weeks, I thought, ever since she left the fair. Her long-lost son."

A wild wave of feelings almost knocked me off my feet. I had a mum! No! Yes! A living, breathing mum, come to fetch me after all these years. Unbelievable! She wasn't dead after all. I'd finally found myself a real flesh and blood mother... only now I'd lost her again...

"Are you alright, Nick?" asked Edwin. "You've gone a very strange colour all of a sudden. Do you need something to eat? Perhaps one of your pies, Mrs Grubson?"

I was dimly aware of someone pushing something hot into my hand, but I was too shocked and confused to even think about food. There I was, hoping against hope that Annie might have some answers for me if we managed to find her again. But it turned out she *was* the answer. The answer to every single lonely night I'd ever spent wishing; every time I'd hugged my arms round my chest for warmth and pretended someone was holding me tight. Someone who loved me. And yet... if I really *was* her long-lost son, why didn't she tell me? Why didn't she scoop me up, there and then, the moment we were safe, and swear to never let me go again?

"Nick?" Edwin's face swam slowly back into focus. "I've been thinking. Didn't we hear the magician say something about a fair? Do you think that's where he's taken her? There's one out on Blackthorn Common at the moment. I've seen the posters."

"Oh dear, I hope not, poor love," said Mrs Grubson. "Not after everything she's been through. Goodness knows what her husband's lot will do to her now. *He* was the real freak if you ask me, that stepfather of yours."

"What do you mean?" There were so many conflicting thoughts running through my head that my brain was having trouble keeping up. "What stepfather?" Oh, wait, that must be the husband Annie was trying to tell me about at the magic show… the man she'd killed in a fire. Of course! "What about my real dad, then?" I blurted out. "What happened to him? And why does everyone keep talking about freaks?" First the magician—*fresh delivery… fair… freaks*—and now the pie-woman.

"Poor love," said Mrs Grubson again. It wasn't clear if she meant me or Annie. "She didn't tell you, then? You know... about...?" She circled a podgy hand in front of her face, her cheeks burning red enough to cook pies on.

"Tell me what?" I shook my head, trying to clear a path through the foggy tangle of thoughts and emotions. Annie wasn't a freak. Not my mum. Was she?

"Oh dear. Maybe I've said too much and it's really not my place." Mrs Grubson frowned, and thrust a pie at Edwin too. It was a wonder she made enough money to live on at the rate she gave them away. "Look, I barely know her, really," she said, "but I always try and show kindness to a soul in trouble if I can. And between you and me, I never met a more troubled soul than your poor mother."

"Anything you can tell us would be good," Edwin mumbled, through a mouthful of hot pastry. "Anything at all."

Mrs Grubson scratched her forehead with greasy fingernails. "Like I said, I don't know much—she only opened up to me that one time, when she was telling me about her son. About you, I mean. And about what happened to her husband. I swore blind I'd never tell another living soul about *that*. But if you're right, and she really *is* back at the fair..." Her frown deepened as she sucked a long slug of air through the gaps in her teeth. "Well, I hope she's alright. That's all I'm saying. Here," she scooped up another pair of pies and pushed them across the counter towards us. "Can't have you boys heading all the way out to Blackthorn Common on empty stomachs, can we? Good luck, my loves," she added as two more customers came into the shop. I guessed that was as much information as we were going to get out of her. "I'll be thinking of you."

It was a crying shame really. Any other afternoon and I'd have felt like a Pie King, rich beyond my wildest pastry dreams. But not today. Not with my head full of a hundred wriggling questions, and my stomach squirming like a barrel of eels whenever I thought about Annie. Every mouthful I took reminded me of our strange morning together—of running through the back streets by her side, wolfing down hot beef and mutton as I went.

If only she'd told me who she was there and then. If only we'd found somewhere safer to lay low. We could be on our way to a new life together even now, away from the coppers and the rats and the sewer stench. But what was done was done, and a pie was still a pie. I forced the first one down as best as I could, and tucked the second into my pocket for later. Mrs Grubson was right. I needed to keep my strength up for the fair. Goodness only knew what we'd find when we got there.

I might not have been to a magic show before, but I'd been to plenty of fairs in my time. They're rich pickings for waifs and strays—full of unwanted food and unguarded punters; a treasure trove of half-eaten treats and fumbled coins. But mainly they're just full of fun. Of colour and noise. Even with so much on my mind, I still felt that familiar thrill as the first sounds of the fair reached our ears: the buzz of the crowds, the whirling notes of the steam organ and the cries of the fairground barkers...

"Roll up, roll up! Come board your ship and ride the waves on the incredible Sea-on-Land! Marvel at the weird and wonderful waxworks!"

I'd never seen Blackthorn Common so busy. The heavy grey clouds gathering overhead didn't seem to be putting anyone off. There were plenty more people streaming in behind us too. But where was Annie? That was the question.

Roll up, roll up! Come find your long-lost mother.

"They've got Platform Gallopers," breathed Edwin, his eyes already glazed with the wonder of it all. "Look at that Velocipede go!"

"Come on," I said, dragging him away from the big rides towards the tents and sideshows. I still didn't understand why all the clues seemed to lead to a fairground freak show—it's not like Annie was a giant or a conjoined twin or anything—but the sooner we found her, the sooner we could make sense of it all. She had to be here somewhere, otherwise... No. There was no otherwise. She just had to.

That's when I spotted my first freak—at least he looked like a freak. I thought it must be the Human Cannonball out on his lunch break. Never seen such a roly-poly globe of a fella.

"'Scuse me, sir," I said, tugging at the tails of his shiny black suit. "Which way to the freak show?" He wobbled alarmingly on his stumpy little legs as he turned. Honestly, if he was any rounder he'd have rolled clean away.

"Sorry, what was that?" He didn't have the face of a natural performer, it had to be said. With his droopy grey 'tache and mournful eyes, he looked sad and confused more than anything. But not half as confused as I was when the woman to his left started thwacking me over the head with her enormous carpet bag. *Oof! Thump!*

"Ow!" I bellowed. "What's that for?"

"How dare you?" she bellowed back. Her voice was hoarse and scratchy, like she'd swallowed a boot brush. "Why, you rude little urchin. Take that! And that! Calling my poor husband a freak just because he's a little on the strong and manly side. There's nothing wrong with a healthy appetite, is there, Horace?"

Horace the Human Cannonball shot me a sad smile and shook his head. "Sorry about the wife," he squeaked, as the blows rained down on my skull. "It's the sight of so many people having fun. It sends her into a bit of a rage..."

Ooof! Thwack! Right on the nose that time.

"I'd make a run for it if I was you. The freak tent's that way," he added, gesturing with a fat sausage finger. "And if you see the Man Who Married a Bear, ask him if he'd like to swap..."

Freak Show

"You should have seen your face," Edwin said, still laughing as we dodged past the boxing booth and the steam swings. "It was an absolute picture."

Charming. I could imagine the sort of picture he had in mind though—that big old painting in the art gallery of the broken-headed soldier: all blood and bandages and eyes swollen shut. I'd hidden out of the cold with my soldier friend so many times during the winter that I knew every single cut and gash on his poor old face. Always assumed it was some foreign army he'd been off fighting, but maybe he'd just had a run-in with Lady Carpet Bag and her powerful right arm swing. *Ow, ow, ow.*

"Look! Over there," said Edwin, pointing to a big

striped tent. "Flauntacre's Fantastical Freakorium." There was a poster of a sad-looking lady under the sign, with white feathers covering her body and a long beak-like nose. It made me feel sad too, just looking at her. I couldn't bear to think of Annie being gawped at by crowds of unfeeling punters. But maybe I'd got it wrong. After all, I'd only caught the tiniest of conversation snatches outside the stage door—perhaps the magician had been talking about something else. About *someone* else. Some poor person with feathered wings and a tail or an extra head. And Mrs Grubson? Maybe she'd got it wrong too.

"Step this way, gentlemen," called the stripy-suited man at the door, as the large party ahead of us disappeared into the noise and heat of the tent. "Come see the Bird Lady lay a real-life egg. Behold the Amazing Levitating Boy and the Two-Headed Dog. Marvel at the Mouse-Eating Man. A whole world of wonder awaits you inside..."

Edwin was already feeling in his pockets for his money but I was starting to have second thoughts.

"I'm not sure about this," I whispered. "We're not

exactly going to find her *here*, are we?" What I meant was I didn't *want* to find her here.

"We've got a whole family of elephant girls…" boasted Stripy Suit, "…six sisters with ears the size of tea plates…"

Could you hide elephant ears under a veil? *No, stop it.*

"We're looking for a lady," said Edwin, doing the talking for me. I was too busy picturing Annie with a long snaking nose like a trunk. "A widow lady," he added. "Someone said she might be here."

"We've got a woman with fourteen toes…" offered Stripy Suit.

"She's got long pretty hair," I cut in, "and a heavy veil over her face."

"Got a man with backwards feet… Pickled monkeys with lizard tails…" Stripy Suit wasn't even listening.

"Come on," I said, grabbing hold of Edwin's elbow. "This is hopeless. Let's go." We'd be better off heading back to the theatre for another scout round. Maybe we'd missed something in our rush to get away from the magician. Or maybe Annie had found her way back to Mrs Grubson's by now.

Edwin shook me off, gently. "It's alright, Nick," he said. "I know it's crazy to think of her somewhere like this, but it's the best lead we've got. The *only* lead we've got. Let's at least check it out now we're here."

He was right of course.

"Thank you, young sir," said Stripy Suit as Edwin handed over our entrance fee. "Enjoy the show. And you," he added, wrinkling up his nose with a look of disgust as I followed behind.

The tent was hot and smelly inside—even by my standards—with knots of excitable people clustered round the 'exhibits', like gawpers at the zoo. The thought of Annie somewhere like this made it seem more cruel and horrid than ever.

The two-headed dog let out a low growl as I passed by with my pocket full of pie and I jumped, crashing into a lady in a blue hat.

"Watch where you're going," she tutted, giving me a quick swipe with her parasol before turning her attention back to the Mouse-Eating Man.

"Ladies and Gentlemen, I give you mouse number twenty-seven," he announced, holding a pathetic, wriggling creature up by the tail. He shut his eyes, opening up his mouth like a snake.

"Why, I can hardly bear to look," said Lady Blue Hat, pushing her way to the front for a better view. "Oh heavens, he's *chewing* it now. This is even better than the Chicken Lady! Again, again!"

We split up. Edwin took one half of the tent while I worked my way round the other, from the Elephant Sisters to the Pig Lady, desperately searching for a glimpse of black veil. But grieving widows were few and far between at Flauntacre's Fantastical Freakorium. My only hope was that one of the other 'performers' might know what'd happened to her. Or at least tell me who she really was.

"I'm looking for a tall lady in a veil. Have you seen her?"

The Levitating Boy bobbed in mid-air as he shook his head.

"Do you know Annie? Tall lady with long angel hair?"

The Human Statue didn't say anything. He *couldn't* say anything. But I spotted a tiny jolt of recognition in his eyes. P'rhaps I was getting closer.

"Have you seen Annie?" I asked the feathered lady from the poster. "Long hair, looks a bit like me..." I was guessing of course. Could be I took after my dad instead. "Only someone said she might be here. Used to be at any rate..." The feathered lady pulled a strange face. Like someone with tummy ache trying to clear out their system. Oh no, wait. She was probably laying an egg.

Cluck, cluck, cluuuuuuucck. Everyone around me cheered as a pale egg rolled down the chute beneath her seat to land in the waiting basket below.

"Haven't seen her for weeks," whispered the feathered lady. "Not since that dreadful night. But I know Mr Flauntacre's been looking for her." She pointed with a wing towards a curtained-off area at the back of the tent.

Now we were getting somewhere. Maybe me and this Mr Flauntacre could join forces and look for her together?

"Be careful," she added. "His temper's worse than ever since... well, you know."

No. I didn't. "What do you mean?"

She shook her head. "Sorry. I'll be in trouble if he catches me chatting on duty. Just watch yourself, that's all," she finished, before breaking out into another long series of clucks.

Beyond the Veil

I spotted Edwin by the lizard-tailed monkeys, having a whale of a time by the looks of it. So much for helping me look for Annie. Mind you, he didn't have to come with me, *or* pay for me to get in. I left him to it and squeezed my way back through the sea of jostling bodies on my own, in search of Mr Flauntacre.

"'Ere, you can't go in there," said a small raggedy boy stationed outside the curtained-off area. "That's Mr Flauntacre's office, that is. Freaks are all back that way."

"It's Mr Flauntacre I've come to see," I told him, nipping in through a gap at the other end before he could stop me.

A tall man sat hunched over a table, his collar drawn

up high and his head buried in his hands. He looked up when he heard me come in, turning round in his seat with a low snarl of annoyance.

Rat pie and ringworm! That was worse than *anything* out there in the main tent.

"What do you think you're doing?" he barked. "This is a private area. Get out. Go on, shoo!"

"I er... erm..." It was like I'd forgotten how to speak. His poor face. That's if you could call it a face. His skin was a vicious blistered red, with one cheek completely melted in on itself and his right eye fused shut. "S-s-s-sorry," I finally stammered, switching my gaze to the table. Six empty bottles of beer lay beside a picture of a bearded lady in a low-cut dress, her facial hair reaching halfway down to her chest. "I was looking for Mr Flauntacre."

"That's me," he croaked, his voice rasping in his throat as if it hurt to talk. "And who might you be?"

"I-I-I'm Nick. Nicholas Nabb. I'm looking for my mother."

Mr Flauntacre gestured round the makeshift room with a bandaged hand. "Well she's clearly not here is she? Now scram, you little ragamuffin, before I set the dog on you. Two heads bite better than one, you know."

"No, wait, please. Her name's Annie. I think she used to work here at the fair. Something to do with your show?" P'rhaps she'd collected money out front like Stripy Suit—I hadn't thought of that 'til now. Or maybe she'd helped look after the animals. "She vanished at a charity magic show and I need to know if she came back here. I have to find her."

"Annie, did you say?" Mr Flauntacre's face paled beneath the angry red rawness of his skin. "*My* Annie?"

What? *His* Annie?

He looked me up and down, his one good eye glinting in the swollen wreckage of his face. "And you're telling me *you're* her son? That little brat of a boy she's always sobbing about, when I'm trying to sleep? No. Can't see the family resemblance myself," he said. "But perhaps you'll grow into it. Suit you better than it does her, anyway."

What on earth was he on about? "I *am* her son,"

I told him. "At least, I think I am. She gave me this…" I pulled out the locket and held up the photograph inside to show him. "That's me when I was a baby. That's what she told me."

"You mean you've actually seen her?" His voice took on a new sense of urgency. "I thought you were just plaguing me. Where is this magic show?" He grabbed hold of my shirt collar and shook me, hard, a sudden fury blazing from his eye. "Tell me, boy," he hissed. "Your mother and I've got some unfinished business."

"I don't know," I lied. "I wasn't there. I just heard about it from a friend." Any thoughts of teaming up with Mr Flauntacre to track Annie down had vanished, along with my sympathy for his terrible injuries. "If she's not here, she must've run away. Up north, somewhere," I gabbled, saying the first thing that came into my head. Whatever their 'unfinished business' was, it wasn't anything good. I could tell that much by the twisted snarl of hatred on his blistered lips. "She'll probably be in North er… North Northington by now, I expect. Yes, that's right. Silly of me to have come, really," I muttered. "Sorry to have bothered you."

Mr Flauntacre was having none of it. "You're lying, boy," he spat, shoving me away. "I can see it in your face. You've no more idea where the ungrateful witch is than I do."

"She's not a witch," I shouted back, squeezing the locket tight inside my fist. "She's an angel. A kind, beautiful angel."

Mr Flauntacre fell back against the table, laughing. A dark, humourless kind of laugh. "An angel? That's a first," he scoffed. "Quite the jester, aren't you, boy?"

"It's true." Even if we had only spent a couple of hours together, I'd never met anyone more angelic than Annie. The way she'd appeared out of nowhere to save me. The way she touched my arm. The soft warmth of her voice. And whatever it was that'd taken her away from me all those years ago—that didn't matter anymore. She'd come back, hadn't she? She loved me. She'd come back with love *and* pies, which was more than I'd ever hoped for.

But Mr Flauntacre wasn't finished yet. "Whoever heard of a bearded angel?" he scoffed. "Perhaps

I should upgrade her billing when I get her back. Once I've taught her a lesson, that is. Reckon punters would pay double to see a beardy freak with wings!" He flung the empty beer bottles out of the way and picked up the photograph from the table. "Look!" he said. "That's your so-called angel of a mother. Not so beautiful there, is she?"

Two sorrowful eyes stared out of the photograph, framed by a mane of glossy angel hair that came tumbling down to meet the thick flowing beard below.

I stared back in shock, my brain struggling to catch up. *A beard? But... but...* But nothing. It all made sense when I thought about it. The thick veil, the hairy hands holding me up in the locket photo. They must've been hers. And the weak, teary father who'd left me at the orphanage all those years ago... That hadn't been my dad at all, had it? No wonder Mr Rodfear said she cried like a woman... "Mum," I whispered, unable to tear my gaze away. "Oh Mum." What must her life have been like all these years, working for someone like Mr Flauntacre? Having people pay to stare and laugh at her? Was that why she'd kept her face hidden from me at the theatre? In case *I* laughed at her too? *No*, I wanted to tell her. *I'd never have laughed.* She could have three heads for all I cared. I just wanted to find her. My very own angel mum.

"And she wasn't such an angel when she left me to burn in my own bed, was she?" Mr Flauntacre wasn't laughing now either. Far from it. "When she left me for dead—her own husband—and ran off to find her unwanted rat of a son? After everything I've done for her," he spat.

Wait a minute, what was that? "You're her *husband?* She didn't kill you, then?" But that meant... that meant Annie wasn't a murderer after all.

"No," agreed Mr Flauntacre. "Unfortunately for your mother, she didn't quite finish the job. And when I get my hands on her..."

"But she didn't mean to." The words came bursting out before I could stop them. "It was an accident, she told me."

"I'll show her a ruddy accident," he said, tearing the photo from top to bottom. "Now, where is she? The truth this time."

"I don't know. I swear." Not that I'd have told him even if I did. "I thought she might be here. I thought they might've brought her here after the show…"

The blank look on his distorted face told me everything I needed to know. Annie might well have been part of his horrid freakorium—before the fire that is—but she hadn't been back since.

Mr Flauntacre ripped the photograph into tiny pieces, letting them drift down onto the ground like flecks of ash. "…And of course the best way to make sure she *does* come back," he muttered to himself, his one good eye narrowing to a dark slit, "is to hold on to her precious brat… Just like I should've done all those years ago."

Brat? Wait a minute—that was me!

He lunged for my shirt again but I was too quick. I jumped back, ducking out of his reach and tearing off as fast as my legs could carry me.

"Stop right there, you little toerag!" came a hoarse yell from behind, as I burst back through the curtain into the main tent, sending the skinny sentry boy flying. "Someone grab him! Grab that thieving rat."

I hadn't stolen anything. *He* knew that and so did I. But the punters crowded round the Human Spider didn't. The merest hint of a pickpocket in their midst brought hands lunging at me from every direction.

"Get him!"

"Stop him!"

"Grab him!"

"Squash him!"

Squash him? I didn't like the sound of that. I ducked and swerved, wriggling and squirming my way through the tangle of legs and arms towards the main entrance. Towards the looming figure of Stripy Suit, silhouetted against the bright sunshine outside. *Drat!* He'd be on me the second I reached the doorway. I was trapped, good and proper.

"Lock the little blighter up and throw away the key!"

I needed a distraction. And I needed it fast. That's when I remembered the uneaten pie, nestling in my pocket. Perfect.

10

A Date with Destiny

I took a sharp left at a pair of plump legs and dropped down out of sight, doubling back towards the two-headed dog. All eyes were on the main entrance, waiting for me to make my final dash. No one spotted me reaching for the snarling creature's tether.

After all those raw-fingered years unpicking old ropes at the orphanage, the thick knot tying him to the pole was no problem. One of the dog's heads let out a hungry yelp as he broke free, snapping his teeth at the smell of meat and pastry.

"Look!" called a man's voice. "Over there by the two-headed dog! Don't let him get away."

The animal was leaping up at me now, pawing frantically at my pocket as I reached in for the pie. His second head slipped back down over his tail, landing on the ground behind him with a soft thump. Ha! Not such a freak anymore. Just a snarling ball of hunger and frustration. And sharp-looking teeth.

I hurled the pie into a group of giggling ladies huddled round the World's Strongest Man. The growls came first as the creature dived for their ankles. And then came the screams. Boy, could those women scream.

"Aaarrrgghhh! Get it away from me!"

Rrrrruuuufff! Rrrruuuuuffff!

"Aaaaaaarrrrrggggggggggghhhh! Help! Get it off!"

"Someone fetch the smelling salts—I think she's fainted."

"Another one down over here. Make that another two."

"Forget the boy, you blithering idiots. Get that mutt before he has someone's foot off!"

Go, go, go! I told my legs as the chaos spilled out behind me. Stripy Suit had abandoned his post now and was knee-deep in fainting women, leaving the exit unguarded. Out I flew, blinking, into the bright daylight, kicking over the Mouse Eating Man's bucket of furry friends as I went. That ought to keep Flauntacre busy for a while!

I felt bad leaving Edwin, but there was no time to stop and explain. I tore off into the jostling throng of the fair, looking for somewhere to hide... somewhere quiet where I could catch my thoughts and work out what to do next. That's when I spotted the sign for Madame Mystica, the fortune teller. Yes! Maybe *she'd* be able to tell me where Annie was.

I hurried inside to find a tall, wiry woman in a black headscarf waiting at a round table with her crystal ball. She had dark red lips and a silver snake choker round her neck, which glistened in the flickering yellow-green of the nearby lamp.

"Well, don't just stand there gawping," she snapped, looking me up and down like I was something brown and steaming on the bottom of her boot. "The spirit forces are waiting. Tell me what it is you want to know."

"I need to find my mum," I told her, taking a seat in front of the table. "Her name's Annie. "She's wearing a dark veil and..."

"Yes, yes, I see it," said Madame Mystica, hovering her hands over the crystal ball as if she was warming them at a fire. "I see a special lady in your life... and the letter 'A'..."

"I just told you all that. Where is she though? *That's* what I need to know."

"Talk to me, oh spirits," she cried, pressing her bony fingers against her temples. She closed her eyes and began to sway in her seat, her body weaving round in bigger and bigger circles. "Speeeeeeak to meeee!" she called out in a strange snake-like voice. "Show me his dessssssssssssssssssssssssstiny."

To be honest, if I'd been one of her spirits I'd have scarpered. She looked like a mad woman. I was just wondering if anyone from the freak show would still be after me, or if it was safe to slip away and find Edwin, when something caught my eye... something in the crystal ball.

"Turnips and typhoid!" I cried out. "Look at that!"

Madame Mystica let out a loud sigh and opened her eyes. "I should have known you'd be trouble. How am I supposed to commune with the spirit world if you keep interrupting me?"

"But the crystal ball," I said, leaning forwards on my stool for a closer look. "There's something in there." Wispy smoke legs and a long tail glowed green and ghostly inside the glass. A round cloud of a body and two pale ears swirled away above a long nose. It was a rat! A big fat sewer rat.

"Lordy," said Madame Mystica, forgetting all about her 'spirit voice' in the excitement. "You're right. All these years I've been piping smoke into the bottom of that lump o' glass," she went on, "and it's never shown me nuffin' but swirls. And now look! It's a rat! A great big rat." She glanced up at me and frowned. "What d'you suppose that means?"

How should I know? I thought, twisting my head sideways in case it looked more like Annie from the other way up. But no. The rat stayed a rat.

"You *sure* it's my future? You don't think the spirits might've got confused and shown me my past instead?" I thought my days amongst the rats were over now I'd found my mum. At least I'd let myself hope they were. But it looked like I was heading back to the sewers again after all.

"Search me, ducky," said the fortune teller with a shrug. "Your guess is as good as mine. Though I'd watch your toes when you're asleep if I were you. Nasty looking teeth on that ball of smoke." The rat was already drifting apart again, swirling back into clouded nothingness. She touched the glass with her fingertips and grinned. "P'rhaps I *do* have the gift after all," she muttered. "P'rhaps I should be chargin' more. Speaking of which..."

Uh-oh. I'd forgotten about that bit. "I er..." I made a big show of feeling in my pockets for a coin, but they were empty, save for the locket, the newspaper clipping and a few greasy pie crumbs. "I seem to have mislaid my money," I fibbed. "But once I find my mum I can..."

Madame Mystica rolled her eyes. "Forget it. Just be sure to tell everyone about the crystal ball. About how the spirits spoke to me. They'll be lining up once they know I really *have* got the gift."

"Thank you," I said, casting one final look at the crystal ball in the hope it might show me something better. Like a teeming purse of coins maybe, or a big old basket brimming with pies. Why couldn't I have a nice warm pastry-based future? But there was nothing to see anymore, just a faint swirling mist.

The Wet Arm
of the Law

The heavens opened the moment I stepped outside—
a sudden deluge that sent the crowds scurrying off
to the nearest beer tent. I was drenched in no time,
my sopping clothes sticking to me like a second skin.
Still, at least Mr Flauntacre and his cronies wouldn't
be out looking for me in this. I'd just have a quick
scout round for Edwin (though if I was him, I'd be
long gone by now), and then make a dash for it. Back
to the theatre. Back to the last place I'd seen Annie.
Even if my future *was* down in the sewers with the
rats, I wasn't giving up on her. 'Specially not if the
magician was holding her somewhere against her will.
Not if she needed me.

Mud squelched between my bare toes as I retraced

my steps towards the Freakorium.

"Psst, Nick," hissed a voice from the back of the Dobby Horses. "Over here!"

"Edwin?" I peered blindly through the curtain of water. A warm surge of happiness flared inside my chest, even as I stood there, shivering. "Is that you?" He'd actually waited for me. Like a real friend. A drowned rat of a friend who seemed to have lost one of his boots.

"Of course it's me. I've been looking for you everywhere," Edwin said, sweeping a river of water away from his eyes. "I'm sorry you didn't find your mum. You will though, I know you will. Only it'll have to be without me, I'm afraid. I need to get back home before all hell breaks loose. I had to see you before I went though. To thank you again for getting me out of that basement. To thank you for everything. Talk about an exciting day!" He giggled at the memory. "You should have seen them all in the freak tent after you went… I was laughing so hard I fell over the…"

But I never got to hear the rest of the story. He was interrupted by a loud cry of triumph:

"There he is! That's the little blighter. Get him!" It wasn't Mr Flauntacre this time though. And it wasn't Stripy Suit. It was the woman with the carpet bag, who'd attacked me earlier. "That's the little urchin who stole my mother's precious pearl comb," she screeched, her fine shoes sinking in the puddles as she tripped and stumbled her way towards us.

"Uh-oh." Edwin paled, pointing to the two soggy-looking coppers staggering along behind her.

"Don't worry," I told him. "We'll outrun them easy in this weather. Come on, let's go."

But Edwin shook his head. "That's just it—I can't run anywhere. I must have injured my foot when I fell. And when I took my boot off to see, someone made off with it."

I could picture the scene perfectly: poor old Edwin sitting down in the dirt, nursing his wound, while some light-fingered chancer like me snuck away with one of his shiny black boots. It'd be funny, if it wasn't so serious. If it hadn't scuppered any chance we had of getting away.

"You go without me," he said, with a brave smile.

I won't lie—I was tempted. But I thought about how he'd waited for me in the rain, with a hurt foot and a missing boot, and I couldn't do it. I couldn't desert a friend.

"No," I said. "We're in this together. I'm staying too."

It was the right decision. Not the best or the wisest one, maybe, but I could see the relief written all over his face. "We'll just have to talk our way out of this one instead," he said. "After all, it's not like we've done anything wrong. You *didn't* take her comb, did you?"

"'Course not!" I was completely innocent—for once. "You were there. You saw what happened."

Edwin nodded. "I just wanted to make sure we had our stories straight. Before she starts thumping you again. Look out, here she comes."

"That's him," shrieked Lady Carpet Bag, thrusting a heavily-jewelled finger into my face. "First he insults my husband, then he steals my mother's comb. Arrest the little wretch at once!"

"Well, boy," growled the bushy-bearded copper, prodding me in the chest with his truncheon. "What have you got to say for yourself? This nice lady claims you stole her mother's comb out of her bag."

"She's wrong," I spluttered. And so was he. There was *nothing* nice about Lady Carpet Bag. "You should be arresting her for attacking *me*. All I did was ask for directions and she started thumping me with her bag. I don't know what she's got in there but it weighs a tonne."

"What I *had* in there," she said, "was my dear departed mother's pearl comb. As you know very well, you filthy guttersnipe, because *you're* the one who took it."

"What would I want with a stupid old nit comb?"

"*Nit* comb?" she repeated, fanning herself with her hand. "Gracious me. If you've so much as *touched* your filthy head with it I'll... I'll..."

"Don't worry, ma'am," said the other copper, the shorter of the two. "In cases like these the stolen items are usually sold on by a third party, not retained for personal use. And, to be fair, he doesn't really look like the hair-combing type." He wiped the rain out of his eyes with the end of his wet cape. "Now then young man, if you wouldn't mind turning out your pockets, I'm sure we can get to the bottom of this."

"'Course," I said with a practised shrug, pulling out my left pocket to show them. No comb. No nothing, apart from a couple of squashed rat droppings.

"And the other one," said Beardy, sensing my hesitation. I was thinking about Annie's locket. What if they didn't believe it was mine? What if they arrested me for jewellery theft? It's one thing to be locked away for a crime you've actually committed. You take your rolls, you take your chances. But losing the only link I had to Annie, and getting carted off to jail into the bargain, would be too much to bear. How would I find her then?

"Come on, hurry up," he said. "I've got better things to do than standing in a puddle looking for lost combs."

"Don't forget to check his thieving little friend too," piped up Lady Carpet Bag, jabbing her finger at Edwin. "I bet they're in on it together."

"Me?" said Edwin, in his poshest of posh voices. "I'm no thief, madam. My father's Lord—"

"Aha!" interrupted Beardy, prodding at my right hand pocket with his truncheon. "What do we have here then?"

"My comb!" shrieked Lady Carpet Bag. "I *told* you. A low-down pickpocketing scoundrel. Lock him up and throw away the key. Lock them both up."

Beardy shook his head. "No... not a comb..." He reached his hand inside my pocket, feeling round with his fingers. "More like jewellery, I'd say... a necklace of some sort... and what's this?" Annie's locket dangled from his hand as he straightened out a soggy square of newsprint, his face lighting up like a streetlamp.

No, no, no. Not the newspaper clipping! That was all I needed. *Please let the ink be too smudged to read*, I prayed, willing the rain down harder than ever.

"A jewellery thief as well," tutted Lady Carpet Bag. "I should've guessed."

"I HAVEN'T STOLEN ANYTHING," I yelled, almost crying with frustration. How was I going to talk my way out of this one? "The locket's mine. My mum gave it to me."

"Oh yes?" said the short copper. "What's her name then? Where can we find this oh-so-generous mother of yours?"

If only I knew the answer to that one. "Her name's Annie," I muttered.

"Annie what?"

What *was* her name? Annie Flauntacre? Probably, but that was no good, was it? Mr Flauntacre was the last person I wanted the police talking to.

"Annie... er... Annie..." My mind had gone blank. *Come on. Just say a name. Any name.* "Annie... Pie." What?! Pie? What kind of name was that?

Shorty rolled his eyes. "And this 'Mrs Pie' lives where exactly?" he said. "No, don't tell me... Baker Street! Bread Street! Pudding Lane!" He turned to his taller, beardier colleague. "Pudding Lane! Get it? Here, what's that you've got there?"

Beardy held out the soggy-looking newspaper clipping. The ink was smudged round the edges, but the headline was still clear: 'Missing Boy Steals Orphanage Charity Collection'. And the picture underneath still looked exactly like me.

Dumplings and door-knockers. I was a goner and we all knew it.

Out of the Frying Pan and into the Fire

"Well, well, well," said Beardy. "According to this, your name's Nicholas Nabb. Not Nicholas Pie."

"What did I tell you?" Lady Carpet Bag was flushed with excitement. "The boy's a menace to society."

"It's not what you think," I said. "I didn't take that money. It was Mr Rodfear. It had to be." But I could tell by the look on Beardy's face he didn't believe me. None of them did. I turned to Edwin—at least *he* knew I wouldn't steal from a charity box. But even Edwin seemed uncertain now, his gaze darting between me, the clipping and Beardy.

"I wouldn't *do* that," I told him. "I swear on my mother's life. On Annie's life."

"Alright," Edwin said, at last. "That's good enough

for me. I believe you."

"Well I don't," cut in Lady Carpet Bag. "He clearly took the orphanage money just like he took my comb."

Beardy nodded. "Cuff the pair of them and let's get out of here, before we catch our death of cold. I'm swimming inside my boots, here."

"NO! You can't do that," Edwin burst out. His eyes were wide with fear. "My father will be beside himself."

Really? Who *was* this father of his?

"Well you should have thought of that before you took up with Master Lightfingers Pie here, shouldn't you?" said Beardy, chuckling at his own joke. "Don't worry son, we'll take good care of you. Free board and lodging, the works."

"W-w-wait!" came a breathless cry. "Stop!"

Shorty already had my arms behind my back ready to cuff me, but stopped at the sight of the Human Cannonball waddling towards us through the rain, puffing and panting like a train engine.

"Thank... goodness," Cannonball gasped, sinking to his knees in a muddy pool of water. "I... f-found your comb... my dear," he told Lady Carpet Bag. "It must have fallen out your bag... w-when you were hitting the boy."

"There!" I cried. "I told you I didn't take it, you old witch. I'm innocent."

"Hmm, innocent of comb-theft maybe," agreed Shorty, giving my arms an extra painful twist behind my back. "But there's still the matter of the necklace to deal with, not to mention the missing orphanage funds. So we'll have no more cheek out of you, thank you very much."

"Excuse me, officers." Everyone turned to see another figure emerging through the clouded curtain of rain. Where were they all coming from? It was a tall, thin man this time, with an oiled 'tache and a long black frock coat, like an undertaker.

What now? I thought miserably. Had *he* come to accuse me of something too? P'rhaps it was someone from Flauntacre's, come to add crimes against two-headed dogs to my charge sheet.

He took off his hat, revealing a bald pink circle on the top of his scalp, and dropped into a low, theatrical bow that reminded me of Žalias. They had the same long, bony fingers too. "If I might have a moment of your time, gentlemen?" he said, his voice as oily as his curled-up 'tache. "I understand the boys have taken a necklace... I couldn't help overhearing. And something about stealing from an orphanage?"

Beardy eyed him suspiciously. "And what concern might that be of yours, sir?"

The man pulled a black-edged business card out of his inner pocket and handed it to the copper. "Allow me to introduce myself. Gilmore G. Graspworthy, of the Graspworthy Reform Academy for Criminal Boys."

Beardy examined the card for a few moments, then shook his head. "Never heard of it, I'm afraid."

"No." The man smiled. A wide, yellow-toothed smile, like a dog baring its gums before a fight. "Not many people have. Unlike some charitable organisations we don't make a big fuss and to-do about our work. We just get on with it... our silent service to society. A service which I'd like to extend to you today."

Beardy sniffed. "All very admirable, I'm sure. But if you're after a donation I'm afraid you're out of luck.

Now, if you'll excuse me, I've had about as much of standing round in a muddy field as I can take, for one day. The sooner we get back to the station with these little crooks, the sooner I can dry my socks."

"No, no. You misunderstand me," answered the man. "I'm proposing to take the boys off your hands. I'm offering to enrol them at the Graspworthy Reform Academy."

"But he's a thief," cut in Lady Carpet Bag, jabbing a finger at me. "They both are. They need locking up. They need to feel the long arm of the law..."

The man smiled again, spit glistening on his bottom lip. "He'll be feeling more than the long arm of the law at my academy, let me assure you."

"You mean... Oh, I see!" That's what swung it for old Carpet Bag. "At last," she beamed. "Someone who knows what they're talking about. Boys should be beaten and then beaten some more. It's the only language they understand. And, what's more, it's good for them."

Edwin let out a low whimper. Not sure if it was the cold and wet seeping through his clothes or the greedy look in Mr Graspworthy's eyes, but he was shaking all over now.

"Tell them who you are," I hissed. "They'll *have* to let you go then." The way he talked about his dad, I knew he must be someone important. Someone proper and respectable who the coppers would listen to.

Edwin shook his head, tears glistening in his eyes. "I can't… it's not that simple."

"You *have* to. It's your only chance." *Our* only chance.

Edwin looked more terrified than ever. But he did it. "Let us go," he blurted. "Or I'll report the lot of you. I'll... I'll tell my father, Lord Strickton."

The grown-ups turned to look at him. At his ripped clothes and missing boot. At the broken glass gash along his cheek and the mud splattered up his legs. At the dripping cap plastered to his forehead and the long, uncut strands of hair escaping out the sides. They looked at him and they laughed.

"I have a *very* high success rate," continued Mr Graspworthy, as if he hadn't heard. "Every single one of my former academy charges is now in gainful employment." He pulled out a smart-looking gentleman's purse. "But perhaps if I were to make a donation of my own," he added, "towards the purchase of a few drinks in the beer tent? Maybe that would help?" He smiled his nasty canine smile. "Please, officers, allow me to take the boys off your hands and save you from all that unnecessary paperwork."

"I don't know... if word were to get back to the station..." Beardy tugged at his woolly chin.

"You can count on my discretion," cut in Lady Carpet Bag. "Let the gentleman take them, I say. Perhaps he can beat some sense and manners into the little ruffians."

"The cells *are* full to overflowing already," piped up Shorty. "And if this fellow's offering to take them off the streets for good..."

"No! You can't do that!" I said. "What about Lord Strickton?" *What about my mum?* I'd never find Annie again if I was locked up in some do-gooders prison for wicked boys. It sounded like the orphanage, only worse. But no one paid me the blindest bit of notice.

"Very well," Beardy finally agreed. "Let's hope you can knock some proper morals into them."

"The harder the better!" cried Lady Carpet Bag as her husband dragged her away. "Twice before every meal ought to do it."

Mr Graspworthy gripped us by the shoulders while the coppers hurried off towards the beer tent, taking my precious locket with them. "Come on," he snarled. "Let's get you out of here before they change their mind."

"It's not true, mister," I told him as we squelched along, hoping to appeal to his better nature. "About the orphanage money, I mean. Or the necklace. I never pinched that locket—it was given to me." Only now I'd lost it all over again. My last tie with Annie—gone, just like that. I could have wept with frustration. "And Edwin's never stolen anything in his life. Have you?"

But Edwin said nothing. All the fight seemed to have drained out of him as he limped along in silence.

Mr Graspworthy didn't answer either. He was staring into the distance now, muttering something to himself about two being better than nothing. About how it wasn't his fault the rain had scared them all away.

"Please, mister..." I begged as Edwin's despair began to creep over me too. "You have to let us go." But it looked like Madame Mystica's crystal ball had got it wrong. I wasn't headed back to the sewers after all. This new future was even worse! Locked away forever, with nothing but the *swish, swish, thwack* of Mr Graspworthy's reforming cane to look forward to. Bet he'd give Mr Rodfear a run for his money too, when it came to a thrashing. Bet those long, skinny arms *never* got tired...

No, I told myself. There had to be another way. I hadn't found my long-lost mother just to lose her again. We'd have to wait 'til Edwin's foot was better and make a run for it. If I could escape from Mr Rodfear, and live to tell the tale, then I could escape from Mr Gilmore Graspworthy too. And then find Annie.

I'm coming, Mum, I promised. *I won't let you down.*

Cleanliness is Next to Godliness

It was my first ever ride in a carriage, but I was too busy plotting and panicking to enjoy it. I was too busy watching Mr Graspworthy—trying to get the measure of the man—to take in the scenery. Truth be told, I was feeling a bit queasy too. All that jigging up and down on top of an entire shop's worth of pies was starting to take its toll. It was almost a relief when we drew up outside a huge, redbrick house.

"Here we are," said Mr Graspworthy, dragging us up the front steps as the cab clattered away. "Welcome to my Reform Academy for Criminal Boys."

I'd been expecting something more prison-like. Bars at the windows, maybe, with a heavy, padlocked gate and five foot railings all round. But it was a normal-looking building on a normal-looking street. The sort of place you could escape from without getting mauled by guard dogs or impaling yourself on a ruddy great spike. Lucky for us. And, luckier still, I was pretty sure I recognised the church at the far end of the road. It was the one near the theatre! If only Edwin's foot was better we could've wriggled away and made a dash for it, there and then. But I could tell by the way he limped up to the front door—his face paler than ever—that we weren't going anywhere in a hurry.

An older boy of sixteen or seventeen ushered us inside, glancing back down the steps as if he was expecting someone else to join us.

"Just the two of them today," said Mr Graspworthy. "Best I could do, under the circumstances. The little beggars all scarpered when it started raining." He made it sound like he'd been out hunting rabbits, instead of saving society from unwanted criminal boys. "I had my hands full enough with this pair," he hissed, prodding me in the back with his sharp nails. "If he wants more he can get them himself."

"Of course, Mr Graspworthy sir," said the boy, locking the door behind us. "It's not *your* fault the numbers are so low. And besides, there's still tomorrow." He tucked the heavy bunch of keys into his pocket, well away from thieving fingers. So much for escaping out the front when the time came. But there was still the back door—maybe they left that open for the servants. Or the windows. Not to mention the coal chute, and who knew how many other ways to sneak out while no one was looking. They couldn't be guarding all of the exits all of the time. Could they?

"Right then, you two," said Mr Graspworthy. "George here will show you to your quarters while I take care of the paperwork. And you'd better do exactly as he says, or there'll be trouble. Do I make myself clear?"

Neither of us answered. Edwin stood staring into the distance with a blank expression on his face, as if his mind was somewhere else altogether. Tucked up warm and safe in his posh Lordy house, most likely. As for me, I was too busy thinking about the small door I'd just spotted, hidden away underneath the stairs. Did that mean there was a way out through the basement? Was that where the coal chute emptied into?

Ow, ow, owwwwww! Any thoughts of escape were interrupted by a searing pain in my left ear as Mr Graspworthy pinched it tight, twisting it round in his fingers like he was winding up a clock.

"I *said*, do I make myself clear?"

"Y-y-yes, mister," I stammered. "C-couldn't be clearer."

"No. I shouldn't be here," said Edwin, softly. "It's all been a dreadful mistake. My father—"

"That's enough," snarled Mr Graspworthy, tightening the twist on my ear like *I* was the one trying to wriggle my way out of his precious academy. His oily 'tache quivered with rage. "The first lesson *you* need to learn is respect for your elders and betters. Which means no answering back. Got it?"

"Yes!" I cried out. "He's got it. Haven't you, Edwin? Tell him, for goodness sake!"

"Yes, sir," said Edwin, even more quietly than before. "Sorry, sir. It won't happen again."

George led us along the hall, past posh-looking

paintings of angels and cherubs, and up the carpeted staircase. We never had any carpets in the orphanage, but the burning, throbbing sensation on the left side of my head was something I knew all too well.

"This is where you'll be sleeping," he said, stopping outside a long bright room, with beds running along the walls. Real beds they were too, with real pillows and proper covers. Been a long time since I'd slept in one of those. There were real opening windows as well—a whole row of possible escape holes stretching from one end of the room to another. "And this is the bathroom," he added, pointing to a door on the right, with a stitched sampler beside it: 'Cleanliness is next to Godliness'. "First thing we need to do is wash off that filth." He wrinkled up his nose. "No one'll want you smelling like *that*."

"What d'you mean?"

"I er… erm…" He looked flustered, as if he'd said the wrong thing. "I meant Mr Graspworthy won't want you smelling like that. Like something the dog rolled in."

Charming. And that was *after* a long, cold soak in

the rain. "In you go now," he said, nudging us through the doorway. "You get yourselves cleaned up—water *and* soap—while I sort you out with some new clothes. How does that sound?"

Water? Soap? It sounded about as much fun as an ear-dragging trip to Mr Rodfear's punishment platform. Only wetter. I didn't say anything though. Just nodded politely and tried to smile, like I was a bit more reformed already. The better behaved we were the more likely they'd let their guard down, and the sooner I'd be free to look for Annie.

Washing turned out to be much less painful than I'd imagined though. The soap felt nice and smooth against my skin (not like the horrible scratchy stuff at the orphanage) and there was even hot water! Talk about luxury. Edwin wasn't having any of it though. He stood by the door with his back to me, like he was too embarrassed to look. Or too posh. He was too posh to get undressed too—he wouldn't even take his cap off.

"Come on," I coaxed, splashing and scrubbing away like a good'un 'til my skin turned pink-white and the floor turned a wet, muddy brown. "We'll be out of here before you know it. As soon as your foot's better. But in the meantime we need to do what they say and keep 'em sweet. Otherwise they'll be watching us like hawks the whole time. At least take your other boot off and give your feet a wash... and maybe your face too. I promise not to look!"

"You don't understand," said Edwin, blushing as I reached past him for a towel and started drying myself off. "I'm not who you think I am."

"What?" I slipped my shirt on over my head and scrambled into my trousers. "You mean you're *not* Lord Strickton's son? I don't understand. First you pretend to be homeless, then you pretend to be posh. What's with all the lies? I thought we were friends."

"We were. We are. It's just..." Edwin finally turned round to face me, pulling off his cap to reveal two long, coiled plaits pinned into place on top of his head. On top of *her* head, rather. "Lord Strickton *is* my father. That bit was true. But I'm not his son. And my name's not Edwin. It's Edwina."

14

A Basement of Bones

"Wh-wh…what?" I stammered. "I mean, why? I mean…" I didn't know *what* I meant. No wonder he didn't want to get undressed in front of me. I mean, *she* didn't. I guessed that explained the lady's watch too. And the lavender smell. And the sing-song voice. But it still didn't explain why the daughter of a rich lord would want to dress up like a street boy and get herself kidnapped by a dodgy magician.

"You don't know what it's like," she said. "Stuck at home all day learning how to be a lady. Having stupid singing lessons and embroidering samplers… squeezing yourself into ever tighter corsets."

She was right about that. I had *no* idea what it was like.

"I'm sorry for lying, Nick," she said. "I just wanted

a taste of the real world for once. Of real life. I wanted to be like you."

"Like me? You wanted to live in a sewer and eat scraps out the gutter?"

"Yes! Well no, not that bit. Just the adventure part. But I didn't know it would turn out like this." Edwina shook her head. "I should never have pretended I was going to my aunt's. Never stolen my brother's clothes or bought that horrible old coat. And I *definitely* shouldn't have gone to that magic show... I keep thinking it's all a dream," she murmured. "That I'll wake up back home where I belong. In nice clean clothes. With afternoon tea all laid out..."

Afternoon tea? I'd have given anything for a taste of her life. Maybe not the corsets and singing lessons but the rest of it. For a moment, I let myself imagine it was me and Annie in the nice fancy house, living on tea and cakes and turkey giblets. Not having to worry about rats, or sewage floods, or Mr Flauntacre, with his horrible twisted face and blackened soul... It sounded like heaven.

"They'll be looking for me by now," said Edwina,

glumly. "When they realise I wasn't at my aunt's after all. When I'm not back for tea… Only they'll never think of looking for me *here*."

"You need to tell them. George and Mr Graspworthy. Tell them what you've just told me. Once they see you're a girl they'll *have* to believe you."

"I'm not sure that's such a good idea," said Edwina. "I don't trust them. There's something strange about this place, don't you think? Why's it so quiet? Where are all the other boys? And what did Mr Graspworthy mean when he said 'if he wants more he can get them himself'?"

"Alright then, we'll call for help out the window instead," I told her. "Try and alert a passing copper. A passing anyone, come to that." I put on my best market man's voice in an effort to cheer her up: *"Stricktons! Get your runaway Stricktons here!"*

Edwina forced a smile. "Speaking of policemen, I almost forgot," she said, reaching into her pocket and pulling out something brass and shiny. My locket! "Here you go. I thought you might want this back."

I gazed at it, open-mouthed. "What did you…?

I mean, when did you…? How…?"

Edwina shrugged. "I don't know what came over me really. It was just there, dangling out of that bearded policeman's pocket. And they were so busy talking to Mr Graspworthy, I didn't think anyone would notice."

"You pickpocketed a policeman!" *Blimey!* I could've kissed her. "Thank you," I said, touching the locket to my freshly scrubbed chest. I thought I'd lost it forever.

There was a knock at the bathroom door and we both jumped. Edwina rammed her cap back down over her hair while I stuffed the locket into my trouser pocket.

It was George, coming back with the fresh clothes he'd promised us. "I thought I told you *both* to get cleaned up," he said, glaring at Edwina. But then he noticed the thick rim of dirt round the bath and the muddy puddles all over the floor and his expression changed to one of more general disgust. "Just look at this place," he growled. "I'd better get things cleared up before Mr Graspworthy sees it. If there's one thing he doesn't like it's dirt. Go on, out of the way the pair of you. Scram."

I handed him back my soggy towel, my mind already racing. This could be our chance to get away.

"No going near Mr Graspworthy's office though," said George as we turned to go. "He's got an important meeting coming up and can't be disturbed. And the basement's out of bounds too, obviously. In fact, you'd better just stay in the dormitory."

"The basement?" My ears pricked up. "Why? What's down there then?" Maybe there really *was* a way out through the coal chute.

George looked flustered all of a sudden. "Rats?" he said. It almost sounded like a question. "Yes... rats, that's right. Full of rats it is. And er... and skeletons."

"Skeletons?" echoed Edwina. "You mean *people's* skeletons?"

George nodded. "*Boys'* skeletons to be precise. And if you don't want to end up there too, you'd better do as you're told..."

We did as we were told. To start with, anyway, heading

back to the dormitory like good reformed boys. I was pretty sure George was pulling our legs—trying to scare us into behaving ourselves—but that didn't stop me picturing it. Picturing *them*, I mean—those little piles of bones tucked away underneath the house. Maybe shouting out the windows at passers-by wasn't such a good idea after all, I decided. We'd be in for it if George heard us. Besides, most passers-by would take one look at the Reform Academy for Criminal Boys sign by the front door and write us off as a pair of liars and troublemakers. Probably report us to Mr Graspworthy for an extra thrashing.

It was a shame though, especially as the windows weren't even locked. A quick hop up onto one of the beds to test them out had shown me that much already. And there was no way we were climbing out of them either, not with such a huge, head-splitting drop waiting below.

"Don't worry," I told Edwina, slipping Annie's locket round my neck for safekeeping. "I'll find another way. You just concentrate on resting that foot of yours, so you're ready to run when the time comes."

And with that I tucked away any thoughts of lurking corpses in the basement—tried to, anyway—and crept downstairs to check out the rest of the house.

The windows in the big dining room were locked tight, and the same in the parlour and library. The front door was no good—we already knew that—and I couldn't even get to the back door past the cook with her pots and pans. I ducked out the way before she spotted me and headed back to the bottom of the stairs, to the small tucked-away door I'd noticed earlier. That had to be the way down to the basement.

After everything George had told us, it was almost a relief to find it locked. The key was probably tucked away in his pocket along with the others, out of sight of any passing young criminals. So much for that plan then. But the thought of Annie—and of Edwina waiting and worrying upstairs—drove me on. I wasn't giving up yet. I crept on down the hall towards Mr Graspworthy's office, hoping to find another way out.

"What? Don't be ridiculous."

I froze at the sound of his voice coming through the heavy panelled door, mindful of George's warning.

"Of course he's not really Lord Strickton's son. Scruffy-looking little beggar like him?"

"Good," came the muffled reply. A man's voice. "The last thing we want is coppers sniffing round looking for missing boys..."

"There won't be," said Mr Graspworthy. "I have done this before you know... three hundred boys and counting."

Three hundred boys? I thought about all the empty-looking rooms I'd seen and the single dormitory upstairs. Fourteen beds on one side of the room and fifteen on the other. So where were all the other young criminals? Where had they all been sleeping? Edwina was right, there was something very strange about this place. And then I thought about the locked basement—about how many yellowing skulls and piles of old bones could be crammed into the space under my feet—and shuddered.

"Of course, Gilmore. I'm sorry. I'm just a bit jumpy after what happened earlier..."

Uh-oh, someone was coming. I looked round for somewhere to hide but I was too late.

"I thought I told you to keep away from here," hissed George, bearing down on me with a face like a wasp-stung bulldog. "I can see we're going to have problems with you." He grabbed hold of my hands, twisting them behind my back like the copper at the fair, then marched me all the way upstairs to the dormitory. "Now stay there and don't try anything funny, otherwise..." He jerked a meaty finger across the bottom of his neck, like a knife chopping off his head, and thrust me inside, locking the door behind me.

"He's bluffing," I whispered, trying to make Edwina feel better. Or maybe I was trying to make myself feel better.

"...Bothersome little brat," George muttered to himself, as he jiggled the key back out of the lock. "They'll be paying *them* at this rate, just to be shot of him..."

15

For What We Are About to Receive

We passed the time until dinner swapping stories about our lives, trying to take our minds off the seriousness of the situation. Whatever Mr Graspworthy was up to at his so-called Reform Academy, it clearly wasn't anything good.

"I just wish I'd been born a boy," said Edwina. "I want to be out there in the world *doing* things. Normal things, that is, not getting kidnapped by magicians or carted off for crimes I didn't commit."

"I know what you mean," I said, secretly wishing the exact opposite. I'd rather be tucked away in the middle of nowhere with Annie. Somewhere nice and quiet—just the two of us—away from staring eyes. Somewhere the coppers and Mr Flauntacre wouldn't be able to find us. It didn't have to be a big fancy house like Edwina's. I'd settle for a proper roof and a fire... maybe even a rat or two if that's what it took to turn my crystal ball fortune into a proper future with my mum. Wouldn't mind a whole army of rats if it meant we got to be together. I didn't think it was possible to miss someone you'd only just met, but I missed her so hard right then it hurt. My very own mother, after all these years—where was she now? Was she thinking of me too?

Dinner, when it finally came, was good. Surprisingly good. Surprisingly generous. At best, I'd expected endless prayers and lectures round the table, followed by the kind of grey tasteless slop that passed for food in the orphanage. And at worst, a one-way trip to the basement with an empty belly. But I was wrong. Mr Graspworthy muttered a quick grace and then it was straight onto the first course. Yes, that's right, there was more than one of them! We had clear broth to start, then a giant plate of potatoes and stew. Don't know what was in it exactly, some sort of meat with oysters and onion, but it tasted wonderful. Edwina barely touched hers, pushing it round the plate with her knife and fork, but I wasn't going to let fear ruin *my* appetite. Besides, the fuller our bellies were, the more energy we'd have when it came to escaping.

"Where are all the other boys?" I asked through a hot mouthful of stew, watching to see how Mr Graspworthy reacted. *What happened to the other three hundred?*

He winced as a stray fleck of meat and gravy landed on his cheek. *Oops.*

"Don't talk with your mouth full, young man. Such a nasty, vulgar habit." He picked up his napkin and dabbed at the offending cheek, like he was wiping away pure poison.

I picked up my own napkin and dabbed along with him—cheeks *and* mouth—to show willing. And then, after I spotted the bottom half trailing in my stew, I switched ends and started sucking all the juices back up again. *Delicious.*

Edwina nudged me in the ribs. "*That's* bad manners too," she whispered.

Really? But what about all that lovely gravy

goodness? Seemed a shame to waste it—there was no way of knowing where my next meal was coming from once we escaped—so I rolled my napkin up into a ball and stuffed it into my pocket for later. I snuck a nice fat potato into my other pocket for good measure, while no one was looking, and tried not to commit any other blunders for the rest of the meal.

It wasn't 'til the maid knocked on the door, making us all jump, that I realised Mr Graspworthy hadn't actually answered my question. I still didn't know why we were the only two boys in the academy. The only two living ones anyway.

"Excuse me, sir," said the maid, with a nervous bob of her head. She was a pale, skinny little thing who was quite clearly terrified of her master. "There's some police detectives at the door, asking to speak to you in connection with a missing girl. The daughter of Lord Strickley—least, I think that's what they said."

Edwina stiffened beside me, her face a curious mixture of fear and excitement. As for Mr Graspworthy, well, he looked like he'd seen a ghost. His spoon hung in mid-air—hovering halfway between his custard-covered pudding and his open mouth.

"Lord Strickton?" he said slowly, as if he couldn't quite believe what he was hearing. His eyes flicked from Edwina to the dining room door and back again. "His *daughter*, did you say?" His voice was little more than a rasping whisper now. "You," he hissed, jabbing his finger at Edwina. "Take off your cap. We'll soon get to the bottom of this."

Edwina did as she was told.

There was a sharp intake of breath from George. "Sh-she's a girl," he stammered, as if he'd never seen one before. "A *girl*. No! If they find her here... if they find out what we're up to..."

Mr Graspworthy lashed out at him with his spoon, catching him smartly round the chops. "That's enough. Pull yourself together, you blithering idiot, and get her out of here. Quickly now."

George leapt to his feet, stung into action by the red spoon-shaped mark on his chin and the urgency in Mr Graspworthy's voice. "Of course." He grabbed hold of Edwina from behind, hauling her to her feet and covering her mouth with his hand.

"Get off her!" I yelled, flinging myself into the fight. But George was stronger than the two of us put together, shoving me away with his other hand and sending me crashing to the floor.

Smack! My ears rang with the sound of hard head against hard skirting board, my vision blurring as the pain kicked in.

"Where shall I put her?" George's voice sounded like it was coming from a long way away.

"Anywhere," came Mr Graspworthy's muffled reply. "Just so long as they don't find her..." And then the voices died away altogether as the dining room disappeared into the blackness.

The next thing I knew, someone was hauling me up and slapping me across the cheek.

"Back on your chair, boy, and look lively about it."

"Wh...wh...what?" Mr Graspworthy's bleached face swam slowly back into focus as I slumped sideways into my seat.

"That's better. Sit up straight now." He bent down 'til his face was level with mine, his stewy breath warm against my skin. "You're going to do *exactly* as

I say. Got it? You're going to go along with *everything* I tell those interfering inspectors, if you want to see your friend again. *Alive*, that is."

I nodded, dumbly, trying to ignore the raw throbbing in my head. It felt like my brain was about to burst through my skull.

"Good," said Mr Graspworthy, pulling himself back up to his full height. He turned to the terrified-looking maid in the doorway. "Detectives, did you say, Mary? Why, send them in at once."

Chalk and Cheeves

A pair of thin, smooth-shaven men entered the room. They didn't look like any coppers *I'd* ever seen. No silly helmets or cloaks or lanterns hanging on their tunic belts. Just normal everyday clothes.

"Good evening, sir," said the first one. "Sorry to disturb you. I'm Detective Chalk of the Crime Investigation Department and this is my colleague, Detective Cheeves. We won't take up much of your time—I can see you're eating—but we'd just like to ask you a few questions concerning a missing girl."

"Of course." Mr Graspworthy's voice was strangled, like he had a big lump of pudding stuck in his gullet. "How can I be of assistance?"

"Lord Strickton reported his daughter missing,

earlier this evening," said Detective Chalk, getting straight to the point. "Apparently no one's seen her since breakfast."

Mr Graspworthy pulled out a black silk hankie and dabbed at the sweat on his forehead. "I'm not sure I can be of any assistance there. This is a reform academy for *boys*."

"Yes," agreed Chalk. "I'm well aware of that, sir. Only we've received certain information…"

Mr Graspworthy's hankie-dabbing suddenly picked up speed. "Information?" he croaked.

"That's right, sir. A lady and gentleman came into the Rotherington Road station this afternoon to file a report on a damaged comb… "

My pudding spoon slipped out of my hand, splashing custard onto the stiff white tablecloth. Lady Carpet Bag! She must've told the coppers all about us, about Edwina claiming Lord Strickton was her father. And Mr Graspworthy hauling us off to his reform academy. Huh! So much for her discretion!

"…Apparently she lost it at the fair out on Blackthorn Common," Chalk went on, "or had it stolen… Either way, it seems the item sustained some damage during the course of events and now she's demanding justice." He nudged Detective Cheeves in the ribs. "What was it she said again?"

Cheeves flipped through the pages of his leather notebook. "Ah yes, here we go… less smelly of the two boys claimed his father was Lord Skipton... culprits escaped by enrolling in Mr Grumpworthy's Reform Academy for Criminal Boys..."

No mention of any bribed coppers, I noticed— maybe Lady Carpet Bag *had* been discreet after all. And I guess Beardy and Shorty had been too scared of getting into trouble to come forward with their version of events. Never mind, though. The detectives were here now. They'd find Edwina. They had to.

Mr Graspworthy snorted. "I still don't see what any of this has to do with me. *Boys* she said. No mention of any girls. What kind of a witness is that? She didn't even get Lord Strickton's name right. Or mine, come to that. It's *Grasp*, not *Grump*."

Cheeves produced a pencil from behind his ear and turned to a fresh page in his notebook: "Denies being a Grump..." he muttered as he wrote.

"But you *were* at Blackthorn Fair today?" asked Chalk, watching Mr Graspworthy carefully. *I* was watching him carefully too, praying he'd slip up and say something incriminating.

Mr Graspworthy swayed lightly on the spot.

"Well?" demanded Chalk. "Were you, or were you not, at the fair? Did you, or did you not, take away two young criminals for enrolment at your academy? One of whom claimed to be Lord Strickton's daughter. Or son. We've reason to believe she may have been wearing her brother's clothes."

"Yes," said Mr Graspworthy weakly. "I mean, no. That's to say I *was* at the fair today. And I *did* meet with a couple of young tearaways." He pointed his finger across the table at me. "That's one of them, there. The other one escaped. Leapt clean out of the moving carriage and darted off into the traffic. Isn't that right, boy?"

Chalk's eyes were on me now, waiting for my answer. This was my chance to tell them about Edwina. To make sure they searched the property from top to bottom. But what if they thought I was making it up? What if George had already smuggled her out the back door, and the search turned up nothing? I kept thinking about Mr Graspworthy's threat… about how I had to go along with everything he said if I wanted to see her alive again…

No, it was too risky. After all, who were they most likely to believe, a criminal boy or the head of a reform academy? "Yes, sir, that's right. He ran off, just like Mr Graspworthy said."

"But I believe *this* is the young man your so-called witness was referring to, anyway," said Mr Graspworthy. "*He* was the one who brought up Lord Strickton, weren't you, boy?"

I nodded dutifully. *Please let them search the house anyway. Please let them find Edwina safe and sound.* "I was hoping they'd let me off if they thought I was a toff, and Lord Strickton was the only name I could think of in a hurry. I didn't even know he *had* a daughter."

"As if Lord Strickton would allow any of his children to walk around looking like *that*," said Mr

Graspworthy, treating the detectives to one of his yellow-toothed smiles. He was starting to recover his wits now. Starting to regain control of the situation. "Honestly, Detective Chalk, you should have seen him—all rags and tatters and caked in grime. And as for the smell... Oooof! It's bad enough now, and that's *after* we washed him down and gave him clean clothes."

"Too stinky to be believed," murmured Cheeves, still scribbling in his notebook.

Hey, less of the stinky, I thought. I was positively fragrant now. Definitely more soap than sewage.

"Hmm," said Chalk, with a sniff. "I did wonder what that was. Thought Cheeves must have trodden in something on the way here."

Charming.

"Suspected faeces on bottom of my shoe..." wrote Cheeves.

"What about the other boys?" asked Chalk, glancing round at all the empty chairs. "I'd like to have a quick word with them as well, while I'm here. Just in case any of them know anything about the missing girl."

Mr Graspworthy was still smiling, even as he shook his head. "That's quite impossible, I'm afraid. They're out tending to the sick and needy, as part of the reforming process, and won't be back for hours."

Chalk looked like he didn't know whether to believe him or not. "That's all very commendable, I'm sure, but..."

"I could always bring them down to the station tomorrow," Mr Graspworthy offered. He was bluffing. He had to be. "Hopefully they won't have picked up anything *too* contagious."

Ahem. Chalk cleared his throat. "No. That won't be necessary. We know where to find you if we have any further questions. Unless there's anything else *you'd* like to add at this stage?" he said, turning back to me. "Anything you'd like to share...?"

Last chance. If I didn't say anything now they'd be off out that door, leaving poor old Edwina to her fate. And what if Mr Graspworthy decided to finish her off altogether, rather than risk the truth coming out? Better a silent skeleton hidden away in the basement than a living, breathing girl, shouting out accusations left, right and centre. In fact, make that two silent skeletons.

"Mr Graspworthy and George…" I began.

"Yes...?" prompted Chalk.

But on the other hand, what if I made things even worse? What if I forced Mr Graspworthy's hand by reporting him? What if George was down in the basement with Edwina at that very moment, waiting for some sort of signal—three short stamps on the floor, or something—to let him know the game was up? That it was time to get rid of the Edwina-shaped evidence? "They… er…"

"They what?"

I must've changed my mind a hundred times as everyone waited for me to finish the sentence. "They… they… they serve delicious food," I said, pretending to suck the last bit of custard off my spoon. I couldn't do it. "That was a *really* tasty pudding. 'Specially the raisins."

"Raisins delicious," wrote Cheeves.

Chalk snatched his pencil away. "Why are you writing *that* down? What possible connection can raisins have to the case?" he demanded.

Cheeves blushed. "I thought maybe it was a clue. You know, like in that detective story, the Mystery of the Missing Sultana." His blush deepened. "Though she was a Sultan's wife, now I come to think about it. Not a bit of dried fruit."

"Dried fruit," repeated Chalk, rolling his eyes. "Spare me!"

He and Mr Graspworthy laughed, like they were old friends, while Cheeves looked from one to the other, as if he wasn't sure whether to join in or not. "Probably currants too!" he said at last, with a squeaky giggle.

Chalk shook his head and sighed. "Thank you, Mr Graspworthy. We've taken up quite enough of your time. I'd better let you get back to your delicious dessert. But if you *do* hear anything..."

Wait, I wanted to cry out as Cheeves tucked his notebook back into his pocket. *I didn't mean it about the pudding. I mean, yes, it was delicious but that's not important. They're lying about Edwina—that's what I wanted to tell you. She's here somewhere—I know she is. You have to find her. You have to save her before it's too late.*

"Of course," agreed Mr Graspworthy, shaking hands with them both. "You'll be the first to know."

Mind the Bugs Don't Bite

I slipped the pudding spoon into my pocket while the maid was showing Chalk and Cheeves out, hoping Mr Graspworthy wouldn't notice. It wouldn't be much of a weapon, if he turned nasty after my raisin outburst, but it was better than nothing. I needn't have worried though. The fight and swagger drained back out of him as soon as the door shut behind the two detectives. He sat there, with his head in his hands, muttering darkly under his breath: "How could I have been so stupid? What if they come back? What if they start digging around? Demanding to see the basement?"

Uh-oh. It looked like George really was telling the truth. But why were the two of them killing off criminal boys and hiding their bones under the floor?

Seemed like a bit of an extreme way to rid the streets of petty crime. And what was in it for them exactly? More to the point, how were Edwina and I going to get away before they did the same to us?

"Gosh, is that the time?" I asked, looking at the grandfather clock in the corner, as if I knew what those ticking hands actually meant. The long one was pointing to the number three and the short stubby one had just gone past eight. "I might go and find Edwina and get off to bed. It's been a long day." I even added a yawn for good measure.

"What?" Mr Graspworthy roused himself from his gloomy stupor, looking up in surprise as if he'd forgotten I was there. "Oh no you don't. Miss Strickton will be staying somewhere nice and secure, where we can keep our eye on her. At least until we've decided what to do... how best to dispose of her without arousing suspicion." He let out a low groan, his head dropping back into his hands. "If only I'd listened... if only I hadn't been in such a hurry to make up the numbers... if only they'd held onto the others in the first place..."

"I could talk to her for you," I offered. "Persuade her not to say anything to her father if you promise to let us go. She'll listen to me, I know she will. And then…"

Mr Graspworthy glanced up a second time. For one glorious moment, it looked like he was actually considering it. But then he shook his head and sighed. "I think it's a little late for that now, don't you? No, you'll be on your own tonight. And no funny business, or else…"

He didn't say what would happen if I misbehaved. He didn't need to. I could picture the rotting bones just fine on my own. Instead he followed me all the way up the stairs to the empty dormitory, in complete silence, locking the door behind me. That meant there must be two sets of keys—one in George's pocket and one in his. But I couldn't see how to get my hands on either one of them, short of escaping through an upstairs window and then breaking back in through a downstairs one… by which time I'd be better off running for help instead. Hmm…

There was a clean nightshirt waiting for me on one

of the beds—the maid must've left it there when she came in to pull the curtains—and by the time I'd filled the chamber pot there was a fully finished plan waiting for me inside my head as well. The windows might be too high to jump out of, but once George and Mr Graspworthy were asleep I could lower myself down, instead, using knotted bedsheets. If Edwina could climb up a knotted rope to save herself, I reckoned I could probably climb down one to save her again. The next bit of my plan—the bit where I told the police where to find her, without getting myself arrested for pinching orphanage money—might prove trickier. But what choice did I have? If they didn't find Edwina soon it could be too late.

I slipped my nightshirt on over the top of my clothes and climbed into bed, feeling as sleepy as a rat with a rocket up his bum. Nerves I s'pose. But I shut my eyes and pretended anyway, in case George came in to check on me, waiting 'til it was safe to put my plan into operation. Like I said, I wasn't sleepy. At least I didn't think I was. But one minute I was lying there, listening to the strange creaking of the house and the scuttling in the walls, and the next thing I knew I was back at the magic show. Only I'd grown a big tangly beard while I wasn't looking.

There was a tap on my shoulder. I swung round in surprise to see Annie sitting there, veil-less, with a matching beard of her own.

"I knew it," she said, seeing the look on my face. "I knew you'd hate me when you found out the truth." Tears dripped down her bearded cheeks. "That's why I left you at the orphanage."

"What? No, you've got it all wrong," I tried to explain. "I could *never* hate you. It was a shock seeing you here, that's all. A good shock." But that only made her cry harder. She pointed to the magician, who was dragging a heavy black coffin out onto the stage.

"Come on, Nicholas," he called, beckoning me to join him. "In you get. It's time to join Edwina in the basement."

"No!" I shouted back. "You can't make me. I'll tell the police. I'll tell my mum!" But when I turned round to check, Annie was already gone. "No!" I cried again. "Come back!" I had to get to her before she disappeared forever.

I tried running for the door—trying desperately to reach her—but my legs didn't seem to be working properly and I kept tripping over the end of my beard. It was *really* long now, snaking along the floor like a strange hairy animal.

"You'll never get away," laughed the magician. And suddenly, just like that, the entire theatre was full of laughing people. There were the two wet coppers from the fair, beating their truncheons against their palms... there was the Incredible Mouse Eating Man, with a rat in one hand and a half-chewed human foot in the other... and there was Lady Carpet Bag, waving her comb in the air like a sword, laughing along with the best of them. Even Madame Mystica was there, her crystal ball balanced on top of her head like a fancy glass hat.

"It's too late. Your mother's gone," she called after me. "Only the spirits know where to find her now."

"Where? Make them tell me," I begged. "Please."

The fortune teller put her hands to her head, clutching at the crystal ball as she swayed from side to side. "Speak to me, oh spirits. Show me the bearded lady… Yes. Yes! I see her now! She's in—"

I woke with a start, heart thumping wildly, brain all in a muddle. Something was missing. The smell! How come the air smelt all clean and turdless? And what'd happened to the sewer floor to make it so soft and sinky? So warm? And then I remembered. I remembered it all: the magic show. The fair. The Reform Academy. I remembered Edwina and Annie, both of them vanished away and waiting for me to find them. To save them. Edwina was still in the building somewhere—I was sure of it. But as for Annie... If only I'd stayed asleep a few minutes more. A few seconds more. I'd been so close to finding the answer. I screwed my eyes up tight and willed myself back to the theatre, to Madame Mystica, but the dream was well and truly gone. *Curses.*

I sat up in bed, listening for any sounds of life from the rest of the house. But all seemed quiet. Deathly quiet. How long had I been asleep? Was it time to go? I wriggled out of my nightgown and pulled back the curtain, the metal rings dragging noisily along the pole like alarm bells: *ding-ding-ding, wake up, he's getting away.* I froze, every nerve in my body tingling. But there were no answering footsteps chasing up the stairs to investigate. The house stayed quiet as I peered out at the deserted street below. It was still night, thank goodness. Fog had swept in along with the dark, clinging to the nearest lamp like a cloudy muffler. Perfect weather for a getaway.

Yes, I decided, it was time. I stripped some sheets off the other beds and got to work, twisting and tying them together. Soon there was a thick ribbon of knotted sheet snaking its way along the dormitory floor. Now to anchor it, somehow, and make sure it could take my weight. I clambered onto my bed, throwing one end of the rope up over the curtain pole, then hooking it back down the other side to form a new knot. So far so good. And then I grabbed hold of the rope with both hands and began to climb.

There was a horrible wrenching sound as the curtain pole parted company with the wall. And then an almighty clatter as it fell to the ground, taking me with it. If I'd been nervous before, about waking Mr

Graspworthy, I was downright terrified now. I lay there in a miserable heap, waiting for the metal scrape of a key in the lock. Waiting to be thrown into the basement like those three hundred other poor boys before me. Would he leave me to starve to death down there, fading away to a bony nothingness beneath his feet, or would he kill me first? It was hard to tell which was worse.

18

Gone to the Dogs

Nothing moved for what felt like forever. No sounds, save for the beat of my own blood throbbing in my ears. I almost *wanted* Mr Graspworthy to come for me. *Wanted* to get it over and done with. Better to face the end head on than cower in the darkness waiting for it to find me. Only the end never came.

I don't know how long I lay there, fists clenched tight with fear, but I must've stopped holding my breath eventually. Stopped straining my ears for approaching footsteps. Stopped panicking, and started planning instead. If I *had* got away with it—if I really did have another chance—then I needed something better than a curtain pole to use as an anchor. Something like... like my bed! Yes! Lying there on the floor, I could see the heavy iron legs had been bolted firmly into place. Perfect. I could probably dangle an elephant off the bed and it still wouldn't budge. I tied the end of my knotted sheet rope round the nearest leg and got ready to try again. *Hold on, Edwina. I'll find help, I promise.*

The window seemed stiffer than before. Twice as stiff and twice as noisy. I tugged the bottom sash up into position, trying to ignore the wild thumping in my chest and the tight squeezy feeling in my bladder.

The fog came up to meet me as I leaned out into the night air. It was a dense one alright, thick as custard, with a horrible ghostly glow from the light of the streetlamp. I couldn't even see the other end of the sheet once I started lowering it down. There could've been a big barrel of razor blades waiting for me at the bottom and I wouldn't have spotted them. Or a black magician's coffin, lying in wait under the window to swallow me up.

I twisted the final loop of sheet rope tight around my wrist for extra hold and then climbed up onto the windowsill, my other hand reaching instinctively for Annie's locket, like a lucky charm. As if it might magically lead me back to her... and to a nice non-arresting kind of copper who could help Edwina. "Don't worry," I whispered to them both. "I'm on my way. I'm getting out of here if it's the last thing I do." Oops. Bad choice of words. 'Course it wouldn't be the last thing I did...

I dangled my legs out through the open window, feet swinging in the cool night air. Not that I could actually see my feet anymore. Everything below my knees had already been swallowed by the fog. Perhaps that was a good thing though. At least I couldn't see the gaping drop beneath me. I wriggled round onto my stomach and began my descent, the window dropping shut behind me with a resounding *shhhhwwwuummpp!* No going back now, then.

You can do this, I told myself as I inched down the first section of rope, my fingers already shaking from gripping on so tight. *Nice and steady now, that's it. No rush. Everyone else is fast asleep.* They had to be, 'cause even after that last bit of window-slamming, there was still no sign of life inside. But what I didn't realise—at least not at first—was that things were far from lifeless on the outside. I didn't hear the barks and snarls from below 'til it was too late... 'til I was dangling there, helpless, like a frightened fish on the end of a line.

Dogs. That's all I needed. Lots of them too by the sounds of it. Lots of hungry snapping dogs, waiting to pounce the second my feet touched the ground. They must've smelt me through the fog. That's to say they must've smelt the stew-soaked napkin nestling in my trouser pocket. Or p'rhaps it was the potato. Either way, I'd seen enough stray dogs in my time on the streets to know I was in trouble. Big trouble. I'd watched them rip apart an entire sheep carcass, dragged from the back of the butcher's cart, like it was made of butter.

Carrying on down the rope would've been suicide. I might not be able to see them through the fog, but I could picture them alright, with their razor teeth and the drool frothing round their chops. *Gulp*. They'd have ripped me to pieces long before they realised there was only one napkin and a spud to go round. In fact, they'd probably just have eaten me instead.

But I couldn't go back up the rope either. It was like my hands were stuck to the sheet with glue. And I had about as much chance of heaving myself back up through a shut window as I did of holding in the warm trickle of wee running down my leg.

Where was my trusty rat-scarer when I needed it? Lying in a basement room underneath the theatre, that's where. (Quite the day for basements, one way or another.) Not sure a dog-scaring potato made for such a good weapon, somehow. Unless... hang on! Maybe that wasn't such a bad idea after all. If I wrapped it up inside my stewy napkin and hurled the whole thing off into the distance, I might be able to wriggle down the rope to safety while they chased after it. Had to be worth a try. With any luck they'd be so busy fighting over it, they'd forget about me.

Thinking about emptying your pockets while dangling in mid-air above a pack of stray dogs is one thing. Actually *doing* it is something else. Trying to prize your fingers away from the safety of a sheet rope when they're frozen rigid with fear is no easy task.

"You can do this," I told myself again, whispering

the words into the swirling fog, like saying it out loud would make it come true. "Just let go."

Who knows? Maybe it would've worked. I never got the chance to find out though...

Everything seemed to happen at once.

"What's going on down there?" called George, as the window above me was wrenched open.

"What do you think you're doing?" demanded Mr Graspworthy from somewhere below my feet.

Good question. How on earth was I going to get out of this one? That was an even better question. Shame I didn't know the answer.

Down Among the Dead Men

"Go on!" Mr Graspworthy shouted. "Get out of here. Shoo!"

It took me a moment or two, in my muddled state of shock, to realise he was talking to the dogs. Mind, I'd have shooed out of there pretty quick too, if I could. All the way to the nearest police station, as fast as my trembling legs could carry me. No such luck though.

There were a few final half-hearted growls and whimpers, and then everything grew quiet. Even wild dogs seemed to behave themselves for Mr Graspworthy.

"They've gone now, Nicholas," he called, sounding surprisingly calm. "It's safe for you to come down."

Well now. That wasn't strictly true, was it? The dogs

might've slunk away with their tails between their legs but *he* was still waiting for me at the bottom.

"Hurry up, you little snot-rag, before someone sees you."

Ah! Not so calm now then. But I did as I was told, sliding and wriggling my way down, my despair deepening with every passing inch of rope. It was all over now, I realised as Mr Graspworthy reached up to grab me. I'd blown it good and proper.

He hauled me back up the front steps, dragging me by my collar. A night-shirted George was waiting for us in the hall, with a candle in one hand and his trusty bunch of keys in the other. He shook his head as he locked the door behind us, as if he'd expected better of me. Or maybe it was some kind of secret signal between him and his master: *What do you think, George? Shall we let the boy live? Give him another chance? One nod for 'yes', one shake for 'no'.*

"Do you know what time it is?" Mr Graspworthy hissed.

I shook my head. One shake for 'no'.

"Twelve o'clock," he spat, as if that was a

particularly wicked hour to have chosen for my escape. "And what happened to 'no funny business', eh? Or have you forgotten that conversation already?"

Oh no. I remembered it alright. *No funny business, or else…* And judging by the look on Mr Graspworthy's face, business didn't get much funnier than dangling out the window on the end of a knotted sheet. Not that he was laughing. It was more of a 'let me lock you up with the skeletons' kind of look.

"Speak when you're spoken to, boy. I asked you a question."

"What? Er, yes, Mr Graspworthy. I remember. You said no funny business, or else. I'm sorry. It won't happen again."

"You're *sorry*. I see. Well I suppose that makes everything alright then, doesn't it?" he mocked. "Run along back to bed and we'll say no more about it."

For a moment or two, I actually thought he might be serious. I was all set to make a dash for it, before he changed his mind. But I was clutching at straws, shutting my ears to the obvious sarcasm in his voice.

"You clearly can't be trusted to do what you're

told," he added, his tone turning grave again. "So I'm afraid you've left me with no other option..."

No! Please, no! I should've jumped while I had the chance, dogs or no dogs.

"We'll stick him in the basement," Mr Graspworthy told George, "and let the others decide what to do with him."

Others? So there were still boys alive down there? At least I wouldn't be alone, I thought. That was something, wasn't it? Unless they'd been down there so long they'd turned on each other, like starving sewer rats, turning on their own young... maybe *that's* what they'd be deciding on—whether to eat me or not. I don't know where the thought came from, but once I'd thought it I couldn't *un*think it. I remembered the Mouse-Eating Man in my dream, chewing on a severed foot. What if that had been a sign? A warning? After a mammoth day of feasting— pies, pies and more pies, not to mention a three course dinner—I'd be the fattest morsel those poor boys had seen in a long time.

Mr Graspworthy dragged me down the hall

towards my doom. "If you wouldn't mind doing the honours, George."

No. This couldn't be happening. Only it was.

George's candle flickered as he threaded a heavy iron key into the lock, casting strange shadows up the wall. Three ghoulish giants loomed up out of the gloom like monsters. But it was the monsters waiting for me down there I was worried about: those living skeletons, hungry for fresh flesh.

The door swung open to reveal a stone flight of stairs, disappearing into the blackness below.

"I don't like the dark," I lied. "Please! Don't make me go down there. They'll eat me alive."

"Quiet," hissed Mr Graspworthy. "I've had enough of your nonsense for one night." He pushed me down the first few steps and then stopped. Had he changed his mind?

"Please, Mr Graspworthy, sir, you've got to believe me, honest I'm so sorry, don't make me," I begged, words tumbling over each other in a desperate garbled rush. This was my last chance. My only chance. "I know I shouldn't have done it, mister, I do, I know that, and I wouldn't have done if it wasn't for Edwina, only it was all my fault she ended up here in the first place. And I have to find my mum, don't I? Well I did find her and then I lost her and then…"

A hand closed over my mouth. "I *said*, quiet. The sooner we're shot of you, the better."

"Mmmmwwwwrrrrrmmmmmmmmhhhhhaaahhhrr," I pleaded. But it was no good. I was done for.

"Give me the candle, George," said Mr Graspworthy. "I won't be long. You go and sort out that ridiculous rope contraption of his while I'm gone. Make sure there's nothing left dangling out the window to draw attention to us. Better check on the girl too."

Edwina! At least they hadn't fed *her* to the cannibal boys in the basement then. "Where is she?" I asked. I tried to, anyway, only it sounded like a muffled grunt with Mr Graspworthy's hand still clamped across my mouth. "What have you done with her?"

Mr Graspworthy took no notice. "Watch where you're going," he said. "There's a bit missing from one of the steps near the bottom." He forced me on, the dancing circle of light from his candle revealing a long passageway at the end of the stairs, stretching off into the damp darkness beyond. Into the eerie chill of silence. Why was it so quiet? P'rhaps the other boys were all asleep. *Please, please let them be asleep.*

"In here," Mr Graspworthy ordered, pushing at a heavy wooden door to our left. It opened onto a small cell of a room, with solid brick walls, a bare stone floor and a single stone bench running along one side. It was cold and gloomy and there was something wet dripping from the ceiling, but it could've been worse. Much worse. At least I had it all to myself. No piles of old bones. No starving boys looking for a night-time nibble.

"Where are all the others then?" I asked, as he flung me down onto the bench.

"What do you mean?"

"The other boys."

Mr Graspworthy looked surprised. "There *are* no other boys. It's just you and Little Lady Strickton up there," he said, "thanks to my stupid brother and that imbecile assistant of his letting all the others go. We'll just have to hope for a decent haul tomorrow or there won't be enough to make up the order." He sighed. "Blithering idiots the pair of them."

What? What brother? My brain was still reeling from the news that I was down there alone—that I wasn't going to be someone's midnight feast after all.

"It's not my job to clear up their mess," he added, his eyes blazing in the candlelight. "Is it?"

"Er... no, mister." I'd no idea what he was on about, but playing along seemed like the best plan for now. As long as I had light and an unlocked door there was still a chance for me. Could I make it back up the steps before he caught me? Or would George be waiting at the top? "Not your job at all, Mr Graspworthy."

He scowled. "None of this is my fault. None of it. If they'd been doing their job properly, you wouldn't even be here."

"Couldn't agree more, Mr Graspworthy." I inched my way back along the bench towards the door. Towards one final shot at freedom. What did I have to lose? Things couldn't get much worse.

But Mr Graspworthy was onto me. "Oh no you don't," he said, rousing himself from his gloomy mutterings and stepping smartly between me and the door. "You're not going anywhere, you sneaky little rat. You're staying right here until they decide what to do with you. As far as I'm concerned you're *their* problem now," he went on. "I've got enough on my plate with the girl. With the police breathing down my neck…"

He gave me one last withering look of hatred— as if I'd brought those detectives there myself—then turned on his heel and went, taking the candle with him.

20

And For My Next Trick

The door closed behind him, plunging the room into inky blackness. And plunging me into an even deeper pit of despair. I was 'their' problem now, Mr Graspworthy said, whoever 'they' were. His brother and his assistant? But what if the solution to that problem was leaving me down there to die, like George's skeleton boys before me? No one would ever know, would they? Not Edwina. And not Annie. I'd never get to see her again. Never get to tell her that it was alright, that I knew her secret and I didn't care. That she was beautiful to me no matter what. It was true. A beard wouldn't make her voice any less soft and angelic, would it? It wouldn't make her words any less kind. It was the person inside that mattered.

Strangled animal noises came tearing out of my throat from nowhere; a whole ocean's worth of salty tears gushing down my cheeks as I shook with misery. After all those nights in the sewers I was used to dark underground spaces and a cold stone bed. But this was different. I hugged my elbows into my chest, pretending they were Annie's arms, holding me tight so I wouldn't be scared. I *was* scared though. I was terrified. I huddled into the damp wall and howled, with no one but Death, waiting for me in the shadows, to hear.

I don't know how long I stayed like that, bawling and blubbering into the blackness, but I must've finally cried myself to sleep. Don't quite know how I managed it, with the hard stone digging into my cheek and the weight of my own doom pressing down on my shoulders, but somehow I drifted off into a dark, fitful dream about finding Annie's bones hidden away in the orphanage cellar.

P'rhaps the sleep did me good. P'rhaps I dreamed some of my despair away, even as I lay shivering in the darkness. Who knows? When I woke up nothing had changed—the door was still as firmly locked as ever—but somehow it didn't feel as hopeless as before. *I* didn't feel as hopeless. I wasn't ready to curl up and die, I realised—not yet. There was a way out of here. There had to be. I just didn't know what it was yet.

It was a rat that showed me in the end; a rat that turned my blind hope into a proper escape plan. They're clever, cunning creatures who can get through the most impossible-looking holes. One minute they're there, scrabbling up a solid-looking wall, and the next thing you know they've wriggled their way through to the other side. I've watched them in the sewers often enough, in the dim light of a stolen match or scavenged candle stub. It's like a squeaking, yellow-toothed magic trick, only without the clapping at the end.

'Course I couldn't actually see this rat in the dark. But I heard it, scratching and squeezing its way through the passageway wall, just above my left ear. I followed the noise with my fingers, feeling along the damp bricks 'til they reached warm wriggling fur. There was a loud high-pitched squeal and then, with a final squirm, it was gone, scampering off across the floor in search of fresh food. It was going to be out of luck on that one.

There was a clear gap between the bricks—big enough to wriggle two fingers inside—which must've been how it had got in. If I was a rat I could've been halfway to freedom already. But p'rhaps there was another way... I scratched at the edge of the mortar and felt it come away under my nail. What if it was all loose? I reached into my pocket for my pilfered pudding spoon and dug round the corner of the brick with the handle, working at the mortar 'til the edges crumbled into dust.

That's when it hit me. That must've been the rat I'd seen in Madame Mystica's crystal ball! Not a sewer rat at all. Which meant there might be a whole new future waiting out there for me. One with my mum. Suddenly I was nothing *but* hope. Well, hope and determination. I was going to get out of there. I *was*. And once I knew Edwina was safe I was going to search every last building in the city 'til I found Annie again.

It was slow work but it *was* working. After a while, the gap was three fingers wide and then four... There was nothing to see through the hole—the passageway on the other side was every bit as dark as my cell, but I kept on going, whispering out loud to myself as I scraped and scrabbled. *I'm getting out of here. I'm going to find her. I can do this.* I didn't let myself think about how long it would take... about how I'd manage without food or drink to keep me going. I just focussed on that first brick, like that would be enough to save me.

The feeling, when I finally worked it free, was like nothing else. The solid wall wasn't solid anymore and it was all down to me. Me and Mr Graspworthy's spoon. I gave the brick a final shove and it disappeared out into the passageway beyond with a satisfying clunk, leaving a hole big enough to wriggle my entire arm through.

My hands were grazed and sore but I wasn't going to let that slow me down. If anything I was working faster than ever now, sawing at the freshly exposed mortar with a new energy that seemed to come out of nowhere. I was really doing this! I was escaping from a locked room and there was no one there to stop me.

The second brick seemed to take no time at all, but it got harder after that, as if I'd come to the end of the weak section of wall. I tried one brick after another but the mortar was set firm every which way. It took all my strength and stamina to saw through the smallest of sections. But I didn't give up. I *couldn't* give up. If I really was going to die down there, I wasn't going to do it curled up in a helpless ball. I'd die trying instead.

There was no way of knowing how much time had passed, or when night turned into day. I just kept on digging and scraping and pulling and tugging... hour after hour after hour. When the muscles in my right arm grew too stiff and knotted with pain, I swapped sides. And when the spoon slipped and I gashed my hand on a jutting edge of brick, I wiped the wet trickle of blood on my trousers and carried on, knowing that every single inch of dust I scraped away was bringing me closer to our freedom—to mine, Edwina's and Annie's. Our fates were one and the same now and I couldn't let any of us down by giving up.

There must've been an eight or nine brick hole by the time I'd finally finished. Just had to hope it was big enough now—that I'd done enough to squeeze and wriggle my way through, like a giant rat. But it wasn't a nice, smooth hole and I didn't have any whiskers to guide me or fur to protect me. The jagged edges of the bricks scraped against my shoulders, tearing through my new shirt and cutting deep into my skin. I got stuck altogether, at one point, wedged in so tight on both sides that I couldn't go forwards and I couldn't go back.

No, I thought, fighting back more tears as I pictured my skeleton crumbling to pieces on either side of the wall. *I'm not going to die in a hole*. I took a deep breath in, ready for another round of wriggling and cursing, and then somehow, just like that, I was moving again. It was like I'd magically breathed myself thinner or something. One last twist and shove and I was through, plopping down onto the heap of bricks with a painful thump. But I didn't care. I'd done it! I was free! Or at least a whole lot freer than I had been. All I had to do now was find a way out of the basement...

The door to the academy would be locked tight

again, so I set off in the opposite direction, arms stretched out wide, feeling along the walls with my fingers as I went. I'd no idea where I was headed but at least I was moving.

The next three doors were locked too. P'rhaps that's where the other boys had been kept; where their poor skeletons still lay, hunched against the wall in despair. And the only difference between me and them was a horrible, flea-ridden old rat. All the times I'd lain awake listening to its brothers and sisters, scratching round the sewer walls, feeling them run across my feet in the dark... I never once thought it'd be a rat that saved my life. Or a spoon, come to that.

The passage sloped up a bit after the third door. And either my eyes had got better at seeing in the blackness or there was a touch of light ahead. That had to be a good sign. It meant I was getting closer... closer to freedom... closer to somewhere, anyway. I tried to imagine making the same journey above ground, tracing my steps through the corridors and rooms of the academy over my head. I didn't want to come bursting up through a trap door in the middle of lunch, or straight into Mr Graspworthy's study. Unless I found a safe way out, I'd be right back where I started. But the passage went on and on 'til I ran out of rooms and realised I was under another building altogether.

Yes, it was definitely getting lighter. I could see my own legs limping along beneath me now. Two more locked rooms and then the passage turned sharply to the right. And there it was—a second flight of stairs with another door at the top.

Daylight came streaming in round the edges as I dragged myself up the steps towards it. Almost there. I was just reaching for the handle when I heard voices on the other side. Low men's voices.

"What do you mean, he tried to escape?" said the first man. "How?"

"Gilmore says he let himself out of the window," came a deep reply. "Apparently he climbed down a sheet in the middle of the night."

That was me they were talking about!

"Well, he's certainly plucky, I'll give him that. Maybe we can turn that into a selling point. Where's the boy now then? Up in the attic with the girl?"

"No. He's got him locked up in one of the basement rooms—he's our problem now, apparently. Says he's got enough on his plate disposing of Lord Strickton's daughter. Don't worry—he'll be safe enough down there while we get some more. He's not going anywhere."

No. They were wrong, whoever they were. I *was* going somewhere. Straight back down those stairs to find myself another way out before they caught me and sent for Mr Graspworthy. Before anyone 'disposed' of Edwina. At least I knew where they were keeping her now. I could tell the police *exactly* where to find her.

I was dog-tired after so many hours spent hacking away at the wall, and my throat was dryer than a barrel of sawdust. But I found the strength from somewhere to slip back down the steps into the darkness, away from the voices. I forced my legs on again, creeping along the passage in the hope of finding another way out. It had to lead somewhere, after all.

I was right. It did lead somewhere. But it was the very last place I was expecting.

Doorway to the Past

There was another door at the end of the passage, and this one didn't seem to be locked. P'rhaps my luck was finally starting to change. I opened it the tiniest of cracks, listening for more voices, for any clues as to where I might be. Nothing. Apart from the ragged sound of my own breath it was deathly quiet.

Go on then, I told myself. *What are you waiting for?*

I inched the door open a bit further. What *was* I waiting for? A bony hand on my shoulder? A carpet bag to the face? A snarling pack of hungry dogs? Whatever was on the other side couldn't be any worse than what I'd already escaped from. Could it?

I squeezed through the gap, listening all the while for any signs of movement, of fresh danger. Still nothing. It was definitely lighter on the other side—much lighter. Weak shafts of sun came filtering through the gaps under a fresh row of doors, allowing me a proper look at my new surroundings. Hmm. Another basement, only no sign of any stairs this time. Was it a dead end?

Wait a minute, what was that noise? There was someone there, behind one of the doors. Someone… or some*thing*. The hairs on the back of my neck tingled, my heart setting off at a fresh gallop. I crept my way along, listening at each door in turn. Yes, there it was. It sounded like… it sounded like crying.

"Hello?" I whispered, cupping my mouth to the keyhole. "Who's there? Are you alright?"

The sobbing noise stopped, as if someone was holding their breath. As if they were listening.

"Hello?" I tried again. "Is anyone there?"

"Please," came a woman's croaky voice. "Please let me out of here…"

I tried the door, just on the off-chance, but this one was well and truly locked.

"Who are you?" I said. "Where is this place?"

There was a long pause. A few more strangled sobs.

"I'm Annie," she said at last.

Annie! Her name hit me like a fist in my stomach. Not *my* Annie, surely? I could hardly breathe for dread and longing.

She coughed twice, clearing her throat. Her voice was still hoarse and husky when she spoke again, but there was a velvet softness under the huskiness now. "I'm in some kind of secret room under the theatre, I think. I've been here all night."

I knew that voice. Oh yes. And not just from our short time together the day before. Something burst open inside my chest as I listened—something I'd stored away, deep inside of me, like buried treasure. As if I'd known that voice my entire life without realising. It really was her!

"The theatre?" I repeated. Was *that* where the passage had led me to? And had Annie been there the whole time? But that was the first place I'd looked!

"Please, whoever you are, just get me out of here. I have to find him. I have to find my boy."

My boy. Those two short words sang in my head like

music. I sank down onto my knees, peering through the keyhole to try and catch a glimpse of her, but all I could see was black material.

"Please," she begged a second time. The black material moved.

"It's me, Nick," I told her, reaching my fingers under the gap at the bottom of the door. "I'm here. I've been looking for you everywhere—ever since you disappeared."

"Nick? My Nick? No. It must be the lack of sleep playing tricks on me. Not enough food and water. But oh, if only it were true. You even *sound* like him."

"It's me, I swear." I mouthed a silent 'Mum' through the door. It was still too strange and precious to speak out loud. "And you don't need to pretend anymore. I know who you are now. I know everything... about the fair. About how you left me at the orphanage... None of that matters though. I'm just glad I've found you."

"Nick?" A gloved hand found my reaching fingertips. A dark eye met mine at the keyhole, glistening with tears. "Oh Nick. I'm so sorry. I wanted to tell you yesterday but I was scared—scared of what you'd say. Of what you'd think…" She squeezed my fingers. "I should never have given you up in the first place. I didn't want to, I swear. I loved you more than anything in the whole wide world. But I was terrified of what he'd do to you. What he'd turn you into. The Bearded Lady and her Human Monkey Baby—we were going to make him rich and famous. And even after you were born, when he could see you weren't like me after all, that didn't stop him. He said he'd find a way of faking it instead, only I couldn't let him do that to you. I couldn't bear for you to end up as another freak in his collection. He was a cruel, cruel man, Nick."

"Mr Flauntacre, you mean?"

Her hand trembled. "My parents forced me to marry him when they found out I was pregnant with you. I wanted to wait for your father—he was coming back for me like he promised, I know he was—but they wouldn't let me."

"My *real* dad, you mean?"

"Yes. A brilliant circus performer and the kindest

man I ever met. He loved me, Nick, and he'd have loved you too. Not like Mr Flauntacre. He only wanted to make money out of me. His own wife, the star attraction in his show." She broke off, sobbing. "I didn't want that life for you. Anything but that. So I snuck you away to the orphanage. He beat me half to death when he found out but at least I knew you were safe."

The feeling in my chest was fiercer than ever. Like a hundred fireworks bursting inside my ribs. There'd been someone loving me all my life and I never knew it.

"But I didn't stop thinking about you for a single moment," she said. "You have to believe me. All those years of plotting and planning… trying to find a proper way out so we could be together again. That's why I set the fire in the caravan, so he'd think I was dead and he wouldn't come looking for me. Not like last time. Only… only…"

"It's alright," I whispered.

"No it's not. It's all wrong. I didn't know he was there, I swear it. I hated that man with every single bone in my body, but I'm not a murderer. At least, I never meant to be…" She was sobbing so hard now

I could hardly make out what she was saying. "Oh Nick. My poor, sweet boy. Whatever must you think of me?"

"You don't understand," I said. "I've seen him. He's still alive." I told her about Edwina and me hiding from the magician, and our visit to Mrs Grubson's. How everything seemed to lead back to the fair. I told her about Mr Flauntacre, about his raw twisted face and blackened soul. I told her everything, pouring out all the madness and misery of the last day and night, even though I knew we might not have much time. I'd never had anyone to tell my problems to before. Never had anyone to hold my hand (albeit under a locked door) and tell me everything was going to be alright. That's what I wanted her to say. What I *needed* her to say. Only she didn't.

"I think they're all in on it together, the magician and his assistant—the one who locked me up—and your Mr Graspworthy. You have to get out of here, Nick. You have to save Edwina before it's too late." She squeezed my fingers tighter. "And you have to save yourself. Whatever happens to me, I need to know you're safe."

She was right about Edwina, I knew that, only I couldn't bear to pull my hand away. Not just yet. *One more minute*, I told myself. What difference would one more minute make?

"Why are they doing this?" I asked her. "What do they want with a load of homeless boys and lost ladies, anyway? None of it makes any sense."

"I think they're *selling* them," she said. "I've been trying to piece together all the little snatches of conversation coming through the grill in the ceiling, and that's the only explanation I can come up with. From what I can make out the ladies get taken off somewhere in a carriage and the boys get marched down the secret passage to your Reform Academy. I don't know what for—to feed them up a bit, I suppose, make sure they're clean and presentable. And then off they go. Sold off like fattened pigs at market. I heard them saying something about a factory up north."

"You mean they find them jobs? That's not so bad is it?"

"More like slave labour, I'm afraid. I shouldn't think the poor lads get paid, and I very much doubt anyone bothers with schooling or proper rest hours either. Most likely they just work them 'til they drop and then ship in a new lot."

"No..." I shook my head against the rush of memories crowding into my brain: the muddy mess in the bathroom... the fresh clothes... the delicious food... the empty beds. *Three hundred boys...* They hadn't been skeletons after all. "You can't steal *people*," I insisted. I couldn't believe it. I *wouldn't* believe it. "You can't *sell* them." And yet even as I was saying it, I knew it was true. *That's* what Mr Graspworthy had been talking about. It all made sense now.

"Come on, you have to go," begged Annie. She let go of my fingers.

"I can't leave you. Not again." I pressed my other hand flat against the door, as if I could reach her through the thick wood.

"Please, Nick. It won't be forever. Not this time. One way or another we're going to be together. I promise."

"But what if they take you away in the carriage, like the other ladies? How will I know where to find you?"

Annie gave a low, bitter-sounding laugh. "I wasn't good enough to go with the others. They took away my veil after they locked me up. They've seen me, Nick—they know who I am. At best they might keep me on here, wheel me out as an added attraction for their magic shows to lure a few more boys into their trap. And at worst they'll try and sell me on somewhere more suitable. Straight back to the fair, I shouldn't wonder. To my so-called husband."

"I won't let them. I won't let them take you."

"Listen to me, Nick. You have to go. And you have to go now. There'll be another magic show starting soon and we can't let them find you here. Don't worry about me. I'll be alright. I'm a fighter."

"But…"

"Come on. Think about Edwina. No one cares about a few missing homeless boys—that's the beauty of their plan. No one notices if *they* vanish into thin air. But the daughter of a lord? That's a different matter. She could bring down the whole operation, which is why Mr Graspworthy will want to get shot of her, once and for all. You're the only one who can save her now."

She was right. I couldn't let them hurt Edwina.

"I'm going," I agreed, dragging myself up onto my feet. "But I'm coming back for you, I swear."

"Good luck, Nick."

I blew a kiss through the door. "Thanks, Mum," I whispered back.

22

It's a Fair Cop

I went round all the doors again—not just listening, this time, but trying each one in turn. The first two were locked. The third opened onto the tiny room where Edwina and the other boys had been held. There was the broken window. And there, still lying on the floor where it'd landed, was my rat-scarer. But there was no helpful passer-by waiting on the street to haul me up on a knotted rope. No way out. My heart sank as I thrust the stone back into my pocket where it belonged, and carried on searching.

Another locked door. My heart sank even lower. And another. Then a short passageway veering off to the left, leading to the stage door I'd spent so long waiting outside the day before. Also locked. How was

I going to save Edwina and my mum if I couldn't even find a way out of the building? Where was a helpful rat when I needed one?

I took a deep breath as I stood before the last door of all. This was it, then. Final chance. This was what it all came down to…

Yes! I pulled on the handle and the door sprang back eagerly, like it'd been waiting for me all along. This room was much bigger, with a huge pile of mattresses in the middle. Strange. Ah, wait, maybe not so strange after all. 'Cause above *them* was a trapdoor leading up to the next floor. An *open* trapdoor.

I scaled the mattress mountain and peered up towards the hatch. It was too high to reach but I could see curtain rigging and mirrors directly overhead, which meant I was right under the stage now. The exact same spot where all the missing boys and ladies disappeared. I thought my way back through the theatre, searching my memory for possible exits, but there was nothing 'til I got back to the glass panelled doors of the front entrance. Oh well. My fingers wrapped themselves tight around the rat-scarer in my pocket. If the worst came to the worst, I could always smash my way out.

There was a broken theatre seat lying just beyond the mattresses, covered in a thick white curtain of cobwebs. Perfect. I dragged it to the middle of the room, grunting with the sheer weight of the thing as I hauled it up, one sinking mattress step at a time. All the way to the top. It wobbled like mad as I clambered onto the worn seat and reached up towards the hatch. Almost there… just another inch or so…

I pushed right up onto the tips of my toes and stretched… and stretched… and slipped down sideways, gashing my leg on a bare ridge of metal as I went, landing face first in the smelly dampness of the top mattress. *Bleurgh*, what was that in my mouth? A stale rat dropping by the taste of it.

I told myself that was a good sign: it meant I was following my fate, just like Madame Mystica had shown me. It didn't improve the flavour, and I still spat it out pretty quick, but it gave me the strength to try again. Even though every bone and muscle in my body was half-dead with exhaustion. Even with the steady ooze of blood coursing down my left leg. I told myself the only thing that lay between me and my future—between a future for all of us: Edwina, Mum and me—was that last little inch. Half a thumb's distance between doom and happiness. I could do this.

Alright now. Back onto that seat—one, two, three, go! I stepped right up onto the backrest this time, launching myself into the air as I went, fingers flailing wildly for something to catch onto. And then— amazingly—they did. Even as the seat went toppling away from underneath me, I found the hard wooden edge of the hatch and clung on tight.

Now for the really tricky bit: pulling myself up. My fingers were tired already and there was no strength left in my arms. But I had to try. No. Not just try. I had to *do* it. I had to summon up some hidden power from somewhere and haul myself out through the hole or it'd all be for nothing. I might as well have stayed in that basement room, waiting for the end.

I thought about Annie sobbing behind the door, and I yanked myself up, reaching out with my right hand for a better grip. I thought about how long we'd waited to find each other, and pulled, ignoring the screaming pain in my shoulders. My left hand found a groove between the stage floorboards and I locked my fingernails down into it like anchors. I thought about Edwina waiting for me in the rain at the fair, and I heaved myself up another inch or so. I thought about her locked away in the academy attic, about what would happen to her if I didn't get a move on, and I managed to swing my good leg up against the dangling trap door. It jolted back on its hinges and I almost lost my grip altogether, but then it stopped. It held. And so did my foot. Now I could push off against it and force myself up, thrusting my shoulders... my chest... my whole body through the waiting hatch, to collapse in a shaking heap onto the stage. I'd done it! *And for my next trick...*

There wasn't time to applaud myself. No time to catch my breath even. I could see a dark figure silhouetted against the double doors at the back of the theatre. Someone was coming. I rolled off the stage sideways, throwing myself down under the first row of seats. The doors opened.

Peering out from my hiding place beneath the chair I saw a tall man in a blue top hat, his face buried in shadow, limping up the middle aisle. And then, as he came towards me, I lost his top half altogether, the seat of the chair blocking my view of everything but his legs, the right one dragging behind the left. Was it Žalias come to set up for his next show? Had he injured himself somehow? Or p'rhaps it was his assistant… I remembered the loud thump we'd heard in the alleyway as they chased after us the day before. The filthy curses. Whoever it was, I couldn't let them see me. I hadn't gone through the longest, hardest hours of my life, only to get caught again now.

I wriggled forwards on my belly, squeezing my way along under the chairs, from one row to the next. If I could just get to the door without him spotting me…

"Hello?"

I knew that voice from somewhere, I was sure of it. But it didn't sound like the magician, or his right-hand man.

"Is someone there?"

I froze, head and shoulders tucked under one seat,

my bum brushing at the bottom of the one behind.

"Hello?" came the voice again. Who was it? Why did it sound so familiar? "Looks like I'm the first one here. Front row seats for me then. Ideal."

I didn't have time to stop and puzzle it out. If it wasn't the magician or his assistant, chances are they wouldn't be far behind, with another magic show to prepare for. The man had his back to me now—had already passed by my row without spotting me—but crawling my way to the door was taking too long. I wriggled my way out from under the chairs and I ran. Ran like there was a whole pack of dogs on my tail. An army of truncheon-waving coppers. And I didn't look back, not once, not even as he shouted after me. "Oi, you, boy. I know you!"

Boof! Right through the swinging double doors into the theatre entrance and then out through the main doors onto the street, almost tripping over the sign advertising the next show. No need for my rat-scarer after all.

It felt good to be back out in the daylight. In the fresh air. I'd done it! I stumbled off up the street and round the corner, in case the man from the theatre was following me, and then collapsed against a pillar box in a heap of exhaustion. And that's when I saw them. Or rather, that's when I heard them:

"I still say we should tell them the full story. Tell them she went off with that academy fella."

"What, and admit to accepting a bribe? Admit to letting that charity box thief go? Let alone what they're going to say when they find out we had Lord Strickton's daughter safe and sound and then handed her over to a complete stranger. Whose name we can't even remember... How d'you think that's going to go down?"

"Well it wasn't my idea. You're the one who talked me into it."

I dragged myself round to the other side of the pillar box, following their voices, and there they were: the coppers from the fair. Beardy and Shorty. What were the chances of that? Of all the policemen in all of London, I'd found the two who'd *have* to believe me when I told them about Edwina. I mean, how could they *not?*

"I know where to find her," I cut in, interrupting them mid-squabble. "I just escaped from there now—through the old theatre round the corner."

"What?" said Beardy. "Who are you?" And then the penny dropped. "Well now, if it isn't Master Locket Thief himself? Or Nicholas Pie, as I believe he's known to his friends."

Typical. They didn't remember the name of the man they'd handed their prisoners over to, but they did remember 'Pie'.

"Yes, that's right. And the man you're looking for is Mr Graspworthy. Gilmore Graspworthy. He's got Edwina locked up in the attic and he wants to get rid of her once and for all."

"Graspworthy, that's it," said Shorty, slapping the palm of his hand against his forehead. "I kept thinking of Grump for some reason."

"Come on, we have to hurry," I said. Beardy looked like he was all set to follow me but Shorty held him back.

"This doesn't change anything," he hissed. "We're still going to be in trouble when the full story gets out.

Might be better for us all round if we *didn't* find the girl in time…"

"No," I begged. "You've got to. You can't just leave her there…"

Shorty pulled his truncheon out of his belt and prodded me in the belly. "I'm not sure I like your tone of voice, young man. Talking back to officers of the law, like that. If I was you I'd scram, before I arrest you for taking that charity money. And the locket. *Twice*, I believe. As if stealing it in the first place wasn't bad enough, you had to go and pinch it back again, didn't you?"

"Please, mister. I'm sure Edwina will vouch for you…"

But Shorty refused to listen. "I mean it. Get out of here before I have you clapped in irons. Should've done that in the first place…"

It was no good. If they weren't going to help Edwina, I'd just have to find someone who would.

23

Here We Go Again

No one'd listen.

"Please, you have to help me. My friend's being held prisoner."

"Get your filthy hands away from my pockets."

"Shoo! Get off me, you thieving rat."

"She's at the Reform Academy for Criminal Boys."

But the only word people seemed to hear was 'criminal'. P'rhaps I was going about it all wrong.

"Do you know where I can find Lord Strickton? Please, mister, it's a matter of life and death."

"Lord Strickton? What on earth would he want with *you?* The cheek of it. Go on, out of the way you little urchin."

I tried posh gents with big white 'taches. I tried

fine ladies in their fancy hats. But no. All I got for my efforts were some clips round the ear and a hefty swipe with a rolled-up newspaper. Time kept ticking on and I was still no nearer to rescuing my friend than before.

"Of course I'm not going to tell you where Lord Strickton lives," puffed a big round ball of a man. Reckon he could've given Horace the Human Cannonball a run for his money. "You'll be breaking in, I shouldn't wonder. Robbing the poor chap blind. Now go on, scram, before I set that policeman on you."

Policeman? What policeman?

Ah... *that* policeman. The one outside that baker's shop over there...

It was a crazy idea. But it was the only one I had. If I couldn't persuade anyone to go to the academy and save Edwina, I'd just have to lead them there instead.

I made a big show of it this time—sidling up beside an old chap with whiskers and a walking cane... opening up my pocket nice and wide... choosing the biggest, fattest bread roll I could find.

"Why, you wicked boy!" he cried. "You thieving

guttersnipe!"

Here we go again. I ducked down under his doddery old legs and tore out of the baker's shop, brushing the copper with my elbow as I barrelled back out onto the street.

"The boy's a thief! After him, officer! Come back here, you little wretch!"

I don't think so, mister.

The copper who gave chase wasn't exactly the fittest of fellas, which suited me fine. I was so tired I couldn't have run any faster if I tried. We panted our way along the crowded street in perfect time with each other. At the perfect distance. Far enough to keep me out of his sweaty clutches, but not so far that I lost him altogether.

I set off towards the Reform Academy at first— I was pretty sure I knew the way above ground as well as below. But then I remembered how quickly George had bundled Edwina out of the way the night before— how easily Mr Graspworthy had done away with the detectives' suspicions—and I changed my mind. Better to lead the copper through the underground passage and trick him into breaking down the basement door. That way he'd catch the pair of them unawares. So I doubled back on myself and headed back to the theatre instead.

I must've been gone even longer than I thought. There were crowds of fresh boys streaming in through the doors now—the odd lady too—all jostling each other and shouting. I pulled the bread roll out of my pocket, waving it high above my head like a flag, and shoved on right through the lot of them.

"Oi, watch it," moaned a curly-haired boy, elbowing me in the ribs as I pushed past him. "I was 'ere first."

"Sorry. It's an emergency."

"I'll give you an emergency," he growled, pulling back his scabbed fist, ready to strike.

"I wouldn't do that if I was you. There's a copper on my tail." I turned round to check the policeman was still behind me, but there was no sign of him. No pointy blue hat bobbing above the sea of boys. No shrill whistle cutting through their racket. *Curses*.

Now what? He'd seen me turn into the theatre, I was sure of it. P'rhaps he'd just got caught up in the crowd. I carried on towards the stage without him, still waving my bread roll above my head like an idiot. *Here I am! Come and get me!*

The trapdoor was hidden from sight now, tucked away behind the thick curtain I'd seen the day before. I stumbled up the steps at the side of the stage, lurching into the spotlight as if I was part of the warm-up act.

"Let's see you do a trick then!" called a loud-mouthed boy in the front row. "Go on, show us yer abracawhatsit."

"You again!" came another cry from a few seats along. The man in the blue top hat. *Uh-oh.* I could see his face now, as he hobbled to his feet—his terrible scarred face. It wasn't the magician's assistant, it was Mr Flauntacre! I hadn't thrown him off the scent yesterday after all—me and my big mouth must've led him straight to the theatre. "I knew this was the place," he snarled. "Had to be. How many other charity magic shows are there in London? Where is she then, you little brat? Where's my ugly, murdering wife?"

Prrrreeeeeeeeep! A sharp whistle rang out from the back of the hall. The copper!

"Stop right there," he yelled as I turned from my stepfather to him in panic. It was all happening too quickly. If I headed for the trapdoor, Mr Flauntacre might follow me down and find Annie. But if I didn't, the copper would never reach Edwina.

I hesitated for a moment and then made up my mind. If I wanted to be a proper son I'd have to start doing what I was told: *'You have to save Edwina before it's too late.'* Annie was still safe enough behind her locked door (*please, please let her be safe*), but Edwina... I threw down the bread roll and grabbed hold of the curtain, meaning to tug it aside and reveal the trapdoor. But it wasn't like a normal curtain. It was thicker and heavier and there was no way it was budging. I tried swinging on it instead—if I couldn't pull it open, maybe I could pull it down—but nothing happened. I hung there like a dead weight, watching as the copper reached the edge of the stage... As Mr Flauntacre limped up the steps on the other side... And then, just when I thought it was all over, there was a sudden ripping sound from somewhere over my head. The curtain tore itself away from its mooring high above the stage, collapsing down on top of me in a suffocating pile of green velvet.

Splhuurgghhh-hhhh-hhhhuurggh! I finally wrestled it away from my face, gulping in great gasps of stale theatre air. But the rest of me proved harder to free. I'd barely got my legs clear, barely crawled across the stage to the waiting trapdoor, before the copper was on top of me.

"Hold it right there, you little roll-robber. You little bakery-burglar. Don't think you can get away *that* easily."

Easily? There was nothing easy about this.

"Tell me where she is, you filthy rat," said Mr Flauntacre, limping to a halt beside the copper. "When I get my hands on that hairy freak of a woman, I'll… I'll…"

"She's not a freak," I yelled, a sudden fury burning up inside my chest. "You leave her alone."

"And you are…?" asked the policeman, turning to Mr Flauntacre, and then reeling back at the sight of his terrible injuries.

"It doesn't matter who he is," I said. "What matters is

that this trapdoor leads all the way to the Graspworthy Reform Academy for Criminal Boys. And Mr Graspworthy's holding Edwina prisoner there."

"Edwina?" The copper frowned. "Who's Edwina?"

"I mean Lord Strickton's daughter. The one who's gone missing. They've got her holed up in the attic but I'm worried they're going to do something. I'm worried they're going to finish her off for good, so she can't talk. So they won't know who took her. So the police won't find out about all the boys being sold off like factory slaves…"

"Slow down, boy, slow down. You're not making any sense. What's this got to do with bread rolls?"

"Forget about the boy," snarled Mr Flauntacre. "Where's my Annie?"

"She's not *your* Annie. She's mine." I turned back to the copper. "I only took the roll to get your attention, I swear. I didn't know what else to do. The police from the fair were too scared to help when I told them. And those detectives, Chalk and Cheeves, they were right there in the building… only… only I was scared, and Mr Graspworthy was too clever."

The words kept tumbling out, all rushed and muddled. It was no good. Any moment now he'd be reaching for his handcuffs and hauling me off to the station...

"Detective Chalk, did you say?"

"Yes!"

The copper scratched his chin. "I know the chap you mean. And you say he's looking for Lord Strickton's daughter?"

"Yes! Yes! She's at the Reform Academy. Down the trapdoor and follow the passage all the way to the end. Up the steps and..."

"I've had enough of this," roared Mr Flauntacre, lunging for my throat. Scarred hands closed around my neck. "You tell me where she is or I'll squeeze it out of you."

24
High Time I Was Going

The fire might've left Mr Flauntacre with terrible injuries but he was still strong. Scarily, painfully strong. His scarred hands were iron clamps gripping my throat as I kicked out helplessly with my bare feet. I couldn't breathe. I could scarcely think. Somewhere in the distance I could hear the copper telling him to stop. Threatening to arrest him. But he kept on squeezing. My vision began to blur as his fingers closed tighter and tighter and…

"HANDS OFF MY SON, YOU VICIOUS BRUTE!"

Annie? No. It couldn't be. Could it?

Mr Flauntacre must have thought it was her too. He span round in shock, finally releasing his hold on my neck, leaving me gasping for air. "Why, you murdering good-for-nothing…" he spluttered, but that was as far as he got. There was a whoosh of black sleeves, a loud crack, and then a thumping sound, like a body falling back against a wooden stage.

"Nick? Can you hear me? It's me, Annie."

I took another big gulping breath, forcing my eyes to focus. I hadn't imagined it! I could see her properly now, beard and all. Her black dress was ripped and there was blood under one of her eyes, but it was the sheer determination radiating out of her that really struck me. That and the copper's truncheon clutched in her fist as she leaned over to check on me. And there was Mr Flauntacre, slumped lifeless on the stage beside her. Was he dead?

There was no time to worry about that now though.

"Edwina," I croaked, the words catching in my crushed throat like spikes. "We have to save Edwina. Before it's too late. We need to get to the Reform Academy."

"You heard him," said Annie, handing back the truncheon to the dazed-looking policeman. "Lord Strickton's daughter is being held there against her will and it's up to us to save her."

"But… but… what about *him?*" stammered the copper, nodding his head at Mr Flauntacre. "You can't just go round walloping people with police truncheons. That's a very serious offence, you know. At least, I think it is. To be honest, it's never happened before. I suppose I ought to check if he's dead or not… we could be looking at murder here…"

"Don't be so ridiculous," Annie scoffed, her eyes blazing, "He's unconscious, that's all." Mr Flauntacre let out a low, painful groan, right on cue. "There. See? Besides, I was saving my son's life. Any fool could see that. And unless you want the death of Lord Strickton's daughter on your hands, I suggest you get yourself down that trapdoor and rescue her."

What had happened to that scared widow, trembling beside me in Mrs Grubson's pie shop? To that weeping prisoner down in the theatre basement? This new Annie was a force to be reckoned with. I felt a sudden swell of pride as she wagged a stern finger in the policeman's face. My mother, the truncheon-thumping, copper-scolding hero!

"Yes, of course, madam," he said, jolting into action. "Right away, madam."

"We need to get you somewhere safe too," Annie added, turning back to me as the copper scurried towards the trapdoor.

"No, I'm fine now," I told her, swallowing down the burning pain in my throat. "We need to find Edwina. We need to make sure she's alright."

Mr Flauntacre let out another low groan, his right hand twitching back into life.

Annie nodded. "If you're sure you're up to it. Let's go."

The thought of Edwina locked up in that attic, waiting for Mr Graspworthy and George to 'take care of her', was all I needed to push past the pain and exhaustion. That, and the feel of strong, motherly arms helping me back onto my feet. "Hold on, Edwina," I whispered, as I dropped down through the trapdoor, landing with a soft bounce on the waiting pile of mattresses below. "We're coming." I rolled smartly out of the way, narrowly missing the abandoned theatre chair I'd used earlier. Annie was right behind me, her black skirts billowing out like an umbrella as she flung herself down to join me.

I could hear footsteps echoing off down the corridor on the other side of the door. *The policeman.* And a horrid dragging sound over my head, followed by a series of muffled curses. *Flauntacre.*

"Hurry," I rasped, tearing after the policeman, with Annie in hot pursuit. On we flew, straight past the turning to the stage door... past the basement room where they'd kept Edwina and the others... on past Annie's prison room... barrelling through the final doorway into the long passageway leading back to the Reform Academy.

"How did you do it?" I called as we ran, the words still tearing at my raw throat. My curiosity was stronger than my pain though. "How did you get out?"

"That grill in the ceiling," she said, her voice echoing off the walls. "The one I told you about, where I could hear what they were saying in the room above. I managed to wrench off the cover and squeeze my way to freedom. It was you that inspired me though, working your way through a solid wall with nothing more than a spoon."

"The *ceiling?*" I repeated, readjusting my course as my elbow slammed into the wall, sending judders of fresh pain up my arm. We were in the very darkest part of the tunnel now, running blind. "But how did you get up there?" I had a sudden, crazy vision of her floating up on a swell of air, like a black-skirted balloon.

"I clambered up on that old coffin prop." She was panting hard now. We both were. "I don't know why I didn't think of it before. I guess it was the thought of you, spurring me on."

Wow! My mother: the acrobatic, coffin-climbing hero!

There was a loud battering sound up ahead—the sound of a truncheon smashing against a locked basement door—and fresh shouts chasing down the passage after us:

"Come back here, you miserable murdering freak!"

No prizes for guessing who that was. The man was mad. Stark, raving mad. Had he always been like that or had the fire done something strange to his brain?

Ow! I went crashing into the basement steps—the

same steps Mr Graspworthy had forced me down the night before—my arms slamming against the cold stone. I turned round to warn Annie, but the words died on my lips as a sudden burst of daylight came pouring in behind me. The door! It was open! We scrambled up the stairs, away from Mr Flauntacre's furious threats, to find Beardy—the copper from the fair—waiting at the top. He must've changed his mind after all and come to rescue Edwina. *Thank goodness.*

"Have you found her, where is she, what happened, is she alright?" The questions came tumbling over each other in a garbled stream of hope and fear, as I staggered out into the academy hallway, squinting in the brightness.

Beardy looked ashen-faced. "Gone," he said. "We caught the lad who works here trying to escape out of one of the upstairs windows on a rope of knotted sheet, and he confessed everything. Said we're too late to save the girl, though. The magician came for her after the police turned up at the theatre. Apparently he and Mr Graspworthy bundled her into a carriage, headed for the river to 'get rid of the evidence'. I was just about to give chase when I heard knocking from under the stairs—thought I'd better check in case the lad was lying. In case it was her."

"Well it wasn't," said Annie, already heading for the front door. "Enough with the talking. Come on! We have to get to the river before it's too late."

25

The Chase is On

My head was a whirling mass of thoughts. Dark, desperate thoughts of Edwina, trussed up like a turkey in the back of a carriage, with a napkin in her mouth to keep her from screaming. Of Mr Graspworthy and the magician bundling her off a bridge into the river in the ultimate disappearing act. *Abracadabra. No more stolen girl.* What if we didn't get there in time?

Shorty came barrelling down the front steps, with George in handcuffs, shouting instructions to the copper from the theatre. "You, take this prisoner to the police station. And fetch some more officers to the river," he added, before clambering into the carriage Beardy had commandeered.

They rattled away at breakneck speed, leaving a

weeping George snivelling his excuses. "It was all Mr Graspworthy. *He's* the villain, not me."

"Stop!" shouted Annie, diving out into the street in front of a passing cab, just as Mr Flauntacre emerged blinking into the sunlight. The driver pulled sharply on the reins, the horse whinnying in protest as it swerved to avoid her.

"Woah!" The cab clattered to an abrupt halt, sending a stray top hat flying out into the road.

"What do you think you're doing?" roared the now-hatless toff inside, his whiskered cheeks pulsing with rage. "You're lucky you didn't get yourself killed. Get out of the way, you freak."

"She's not a freak," I yelled back, ignoring the pain in my throat. "She's my mum. And this is a matter of life and death. If you don't get out of this carriage this instant, you'll have Lord Strickton to answer to."

It worked! The old fella was too shocked to argue. Or maybe he'd just noticed his missing hat, rolling off along the street without him. He climbed down out of the cab after it, and we scrambled up to take his place. But we weren't alone.

"You won't get away from me this time," hissed Mr Flauntacre, grabbing hold of Annie's skirts as she climbed in. "I'll make you pay for what you did to me."

"How about what you did to *me?*" she hissed back, kicking her leg out in an effort to shake him off. "Treating me like an animal to be stared at in the zoo. *You're* the only animal round here. I'm through with being scared of you though. I'm through with being scared of anything. To the river!" she called up to the driver, with a final sideways knee-shove that sent her husband sprawling backwards onto the cobbles. "Hurry!"

It was my second ever ride in a carriage, but there was *definitely* no question of admiring the scenery this time. It was flying past too bone-shakingly quickly for that. The driver had taken Annie at her word, whipping the horse on, faster and faster. Besides, I was too busy worrying about Edwina. What if the coppers were too late? What if the magician and Mr Graspworthy managed to fight them off?

Boom! There was a sudden bang, an almighty puff of smoke, and the road in front of us disappeared in a swirling cloud of white.

Rice pudding and rickets! What was that?

"Woah girl, steady now," called the driver as the horse started in fright. "Easy does it."

I found myself clinging on tight to Annie's arm as we swerved wildly off to one side.

"It's alright, Nick," she said, her voice soft and comforting as an angel. "I've got you."

And then the driver regained control and we were back on the straight again, easing down to a slow trot… to a gentle walk…

"Help!" came a muffled cry from the smoking road ahead. "Please, help me!"

Edwina. The sound of her terrified voice sent chills snaking down my back. But at least that meant we were gaining on them. They couldn't be far away now.

"Keep going," I told the driver. "Fast as you can. We'll pay double," I promised, hoping the contents of Annie's purse would cover it. "Triple. Look, the smoke's beginning to clear already. We'll be fine."

It was true. I could make out the hazy outline of another carriage up ahead as the driver hurried the horse on again. Or what was left of the carriage, anyway. Judging by the stray wheel lying on the other side of the road, they must have collided with something in the confusion. A pillar box, by the looks of it. For a moment, I thought it might be the magician's carriage. Maybe Edwina was hurt—that's why she was calling for help. But then I spotted a dazed-looking Beardy lumbering out of the wreckage towards us, muttering something about a magic ball of smoke, and my heart did a double flip inside my chest. At least Edwina hadn't been inside—that was something. But how were the police going to catch them now? It looked like we were her only hope.

The driver picked up speed as we cleared the last of the swirling smoke and turned onto a long straight stretch of road.

"There they are!" called Annie. "I can see them."

Yes, I could see them too. Žalias was perched up in the driver's seat in his full magic outfit, shouting to the horse to hurry up. What had happened to his usual driver? The one he paid extra to for his continued discretion? P'rhaps this was too much even for him.

P'rhaps the magician couldn't risk *anyone* seeing what they were up to this time... what they were about to do... But that was good news for us—Žalias' slapdash driving skills were no match for our cabbie's. We were gaining on them now, the distance between us shortening with every strike of the horse's hooves against the cobbles.

"Help!"

And there was Edwina, leaning out of the carriage, waving desperately. If they *had* trussed her up like a turkey, they hadn't done a very good job of it. P'rhaps they'd been in too much of a hurry with the net closing in on them. But even as I watched, thin, bony hands reached over to yank her back. *Mr Graspworthy!*

"Get off m—" came her strangled cry. And then nothing. What was he doing to her in there?

"That carriage up ahead," I barked at the driver, the beginnings of a plan starting to form. "Can you get alongside them?"

He shook his head. "Too dangerous."

"Please," I begged. "There's no traffic coming the other way. We'll pay you double-triple. If not for me then for my poor widowed mother."

"Alright," he agreed with a sigh. "I never could say 'no' to a grieving widow. Beard or no beard. *Giddy up!*" he cried, whipping the horse on faster than ever.

The gap was really closing in now, my heart hammering in time with the horse's hooves as houses and trees whooshed past at terrifying speed. And then we were moving out onto the other side of the road as we began to draw level... With any luck, Edwina would be able to leap straight from her carriage to ours. To safety. That was the idea, anyway.

I hadn't counted on Mr Graspworthy though. He wasn't going to give her up without a fight, was he? I could see them as clear as anything now, locked in a futile struggle as Edwina fought to free herself from his steely grip. It was no good. She didn't stand a chance. But maybe the two of us together would have more luck... We might have admitted defeat at the fair, what with Edwina's swollen ankle and the police just a shout away, but things were different now. We had the law on our side this time, for one thing. And the threat of a one-way trip to the bottom of the river for my friend meant I was willing to try anything.

"No, Nick," said Annie, as she realised what I was planning. "It's too dangerous. Let *me* go."

I shook my head. "Your skirts might catch in the wheel. This is the only way. Don't worry, I know what I'm doing. I've got circus blood in my veins, remember. I'll be fine," I assured her, hoping my dad had been an acrobat rather than a clown.

My shaking legs felt like they belonged to someone else as I dropped down into a low crouch.

You can do this, I told myself, getting ready to leap. *Don't think about your foot catching in the wheel and getting crushed between the two carriages. Don't think about the hard cobbles waiting for you if you fall. Waiting to crack you open like an egg…* Too late. I'd already thought it.

"Be careful Nick," Annie begged. "I love you. I've always loved you."

And that, it turned out, was all I needed. I leapt towards the other carriage, carried across on the wings of my mother's love. Angel wings.

I misjudged my landing, arms flailing as I teetered

on the edge. For a moment there was nothing between me and the crush of spinning wheels and head-splitting stone below, and then… and then somehow I regained my balance, tumbling forwards into the carriage with a giddy rush of relief. I'd done it! So far so good.

"Get your hands off my friend," I roared, lunging at Mr Graspworthy. "It's all over now. Give yourself up."

"Never," he shouted back, releasing Edwina to lock his bony fingers round my wild fists. "This is all your fault, you nasty little gutter rat. Why did you have to go and ruin everything?"

"Quick. Now's your chance," I told Edwina. "I've got him. Jump over into our carriage. Mum'll catch you."

"I can't," she cried. "Not without you."

"You're the one they want," I said, as a look of horrified realisation dawned on Mr Graspworthy's face. As he clocked that his prisoner was at risk of slipping away. "You're the one who's in danger. Once you're safe, it's all over. The game's up. Trust me!"

But still she hesitated. "Hurry," I shouted, as Mr Graspworthy dropped hold of my wrists to catch her.

"Go, go, go!"

Now it was me clutching at him, trying to hold him back, as Edwina wriggled out of his reach and got ready to jump.

"I don't think I can," she called out. "We're going too fast."

"If you can pickpocket a policeman, you can do this," I told her. "Trust me," I said again. "You can do anything."

"Alright," she said. "Wish me luck."

"Nooo!" cried Mr Graspworthy, as Edwina launched herself out of the carriage.

Boom! There was another sudden bang, ear-shatteringly close this time, and she vanished into a solid cloud of smoke. *Everything* vanished into the smoke. The magician was up to his tricks again, but it was too late. At least I hoped it was. I hoped Edwina was there with Annie now, being helped into her seat.

But it wasn't over for me. Not yet.

"You'll pay for this," spluttered Mr Graspworthy, launching himself at me with fresh fury, in a smoke-blind tangle of limbs and fists.

Oof! Ow! Ouch!

I gave as good as I got, shielding my face with my arms as I kicked back with my bare feet. But he was strong. Too strong to stop as he pushed me back across the narrow carriage floor, blows raining down on me like a hailstorm of fists. Back I went, sliding helplessly across the floor and… and then there *was* no more floor. There was nothing under my head and shoulders now, I realised with a sudden lurch of panic. Nothing but a rushing whoosh of air as my hands clawed uselessly at his flapping coat, trying to drag myself back into the carriage.

But Mr Graspworthy was having none of it. There wasn't even time for my life to flash before my eyes. One moment I was there, my fingers clutching at buttons and hems—at anything that might save me—and the next it was all over. A final shove, and I was gone.

There was a horrid whoosh of wind and wheels, the sound of my own scream echoing round my skull. And then nothing.

26

Welcome to the Afterlife

Gravy. That's what I could smell. *Mmmmm.* Heaven.

"He's coming round." A muffled lady's voice. The soft, gravy-scented cloud I was lying on floated slowly towards her words. "Stand back and give him some air."

It took me a long time to prise my eyelids open. And when I did, everything was strange and blurry. There was a bright shape like a… yes, like an angel leaning over me. But the light behind her was too strong. I shut my eyes again, and dark memories came trickling back into my brain: Annie. The passage. The carriage chase. Falling. I didn't remember anything after that. I guess there *was* nothing after that. Goodbye Nicholas Nabb. The end.

But wait. Would there still be pains running through

my body if I was dead? Would my head still feel like it'd been crushed in a vice?

But if I *wasn't*—if I'd somehow survived my fall from a speeding carriage—then what was I doing in heaven? Unless...

"It's alright, Nick," said the angel. Only it wasn't an angel after all. My heart jumped inside my bruised ribs. I *knew* that voice.

I opened my eyes the tiniest of cracks and took another look. Yes, there she was. My beautiful bearded angel mum. I could see other faces too now... a grinning girl in a lace-ruffled dress... and a policeman who looked a lot like Beardy, except for the smile. Why would a copper be smiling at *me?*

"Oh Nick," said Annie. "You had us so worried. The doctor said if you didn't wake up soon then you might never... oh, but you have! That's all that matters!"

What? How long had I been asleep for?

She reached out and squeezed my hand. No gloves this time, but beautiful furry soft skin. "Everything's going to be alright now though. You just need to concentrate on getting better."

"Where am I?" There was still so much I didn't understand.

"You're back in the Reform Academy, Nick," she said, gently.

Really? I turned my head to the side, ignoring the shooting pains in my skull. Ah yes—I could see the other beds now. And there was the window with the torn-off curtain pole.

"It was the best place we could think of," she added, "while you were recovering from your injuries. And it's not like anyone else will be needing it for a while. Not with Mr Graspworthy and the magician safely behind bars. Hopefully they'll be able to track down all the lost ladies and missing boys now too."

Behind bars? I really *had* missed a lot. "And Edwina? Where's Edwina?"

Annie's smile lit up her whole face, making her dark eyes sparkle. The bearded lady in Mr Flauntacre's photograph had been a poor, sad-looking woman, hiding behind her own hair in shame. But this Annie— my Annie—was all light and happiness. I liked this version a whole lot more. "She's right here, Nick."

"Don't you recognise me?" giggled the girl in the lace-ruffled dress.

Teacakes and typhus! It was Edwina!

"You er… you look a bit different to the last time I saw you," I stammered.

"Leaping out of a moving carriage, you mean? Yes, I'm not sure I'll be doing *that* again in a hurry! Not if Father's got anything to do with it, anyway. It was rather thrilling though, looking back on it now," she added with a sly grin. "All of it, I mean. The whole adventure. But I wouldn't be here to enjoy the memories if it wasn't for you. You saved my life, Nick. I'll never forget it. And nor will Father."

"Anytime," I said, grinning back at her. But the smile withered on my lips as I remembered Mr Flauntacre. It wasn't over yet, was it? Was that what the policeman was doing there? Had he come to arrest Annie for the fire? For the truncheon attack? Or maybe *I* was the one under arrest for the stolen orphanage money? I'd forgotten about that as well.

"What is it?" asked Edwina. "What's wrong? Should I fetch the doctor back?"

I shook my head. "No, no need for that. I'm fine. Only… only what about Mr Flauntacre? What happened to him?" There was no point putting it off any longer.

"I don't think he'll be bothering you again," piped up the policeman, stepping forward. It really *was* Beardy. "Not now Lord Strickton's lawyers have stepped in. It turns out your mother's marriage wasn't even legal."

What? "You mean he's not my stepfather after all?"

"And it looks like he never reported the fire, either," whispered Annie, pretending to straighten my pillow. "Fairground folk can be a bit funny about the police sometimes. I guess he'd rather deal with me himself than risk losing his star attraction to a prison cell. I'm in the clear." She planted a soft motherly kiss on the side of my cheek, her beard tickling my skin.

She might be in the clear, but I wasn't.

"So is it me you've come to arrest?"

"Arrest you?" repeated Beardy.

"Of course not," said Edwina, answering for him. "He's here to present you with your reward. And to keep an eye on me, of course. No more sneaking out on my own anymore I'm afraid..."

Huh? "What reward?"

Edwina was beside herself with excitement now. "The one Father offered for my safe return. And it's all yours! It means you won't have to live in the sewers anymore. You can start a new life in the country, just like you wanted... as long as I get to come and visit." She grinned. "When I'm not busy with my new mathematics and fencing lessons, that is. I still need to talk Father round but I'm not taking 'no' for an answer this time. No more 'good little girl' for me. And no more singing and sewing!"

Money from a lord? It was almost too much to take in. Annie was finally safe and so was Edwina. I pinched myself under the bedclothes to check I wasn't dreaming. *Ow.* No, definitely not a dream. It was all true! No more stolen scraps and rats nibbling at my toes while I was trying to sleep. No more sewer stench. From here on in it'd be warm beds and warm dinners. Pies, pies and more pies. It couldn't have been more perfect. Except for that pesky newspaper cutting...

"What about the orphanage charity box?" I whispered back. "Do they still think that was me?"

Beardy must've heard. He cleared his throat and scratched nervously at the end of his nose. "Well now," he said. "I have it on good authority that the theft of orphanage funds was nothing to do with you. And if Lord Strickton's daughter is prepared to vouch for your good character, then that's enough for us. On the understanding that... er... that there's no more talk of money exchanging hands at the fair..."

"Money?" I must've still been a bit groggy after my fall. I didn't know what he was on about.

Edwina came to my rescue. "What he means, Nick, is that he and his friend will make all that business with the charity box go away, so long as we promise not to say anything about Mr Graspworthy bribing them."

Ah. *Now* I understood. I nodded, happily. That worked for me.

"Feel free to tell everyone about the daring rescue bit though," said Beardy. "The bit where we chased the perpetrators down without any thought whatsoever for our personal safety, battling smoke balls and magic in our effort to save your friend. And the bit where our quick thinking in summoning extra officers to the river led to the eventual capture of said perpetrators." He smiled sheepishly. "I'm only sorry we didn't come straight away. When you first told us. That was cowardly, and I'm ashamed to think I put my own reputation before Miss Strickton's safety."

Edwina just grinned—she didn't seem the slightest bit bothered. But Mum laid her hand on the copper's arm. "You came through in the end. That's all that matters. That makes you a hero in my book."

Beardy blushed, his cheeks turning a bright burning red.

"Well now. That's very good of you to say so, madam. And if there's ever anything I can do for you or young Nick here, you just say the word. The world can be a cruel place sometimes." *For a bearded woman.* He didn't need to say it—we all knew what he meant.

"Thank you," said Mum. "You're right, the world *can* be a cruel place. But only if you let it. And I refuse to do that anymore. If people can't see beyond my appearance then that's their loss. No more veils and gloves for me from now on. I refuse to apologise for who I am."

My heart swelled with pride. How did a sewer orphan like me end up with such a brave, brilliant mother?

"But maybe you can keep an eye on my old friends at the Freakorium for me, when the fair's in town," she said. "Make sure Mr Flauntacre's treating them properly."

"Don't you worry about that, madam. He'll be nice as pie from now on or he'll have me to deal with. If he so much as steps out of line…"

Nice as pie? I never got to hear what would happen to Mr Flauntacre if he didn't behave himself, because I'd just had a horrible thought. Maybe my longed-for new life away from the city wasn't such a happy ending after all. "Wait!" I cried out. "Do they even *have* pie shops in the countryside?"

Annie laughed. "Don't worry," she said. "I'll have Mrs Grubson give me her recipes before we go... And I'll make you all the pies you could ask for, I promise.

That's what mums are for."

"Oh yes, the pies!" cut in Edwina. "I almost forgot! We stopped off at Mrs Grubson's on the way and got you these." She picked up a basket from the floor. A brimming basket of warm pastry. Now *that's* what I called a reward. My stomach rumbled in anticipation. I *knew* I could smell gravy!

Mmm, yes, I was right the first time, I realised, as I licked my lips, enjoying the crumbling bite of buttery pastry between my teeth, the warm ooze of rich gravy and tender melting meat… This really *was* heaven.

I ate three in a row. One mutton, one eel, and a beef. And then I lay back on my soft pillow, closed my eyes, and let the taste of hot meat and happiness wash over me.

"Who knows," Annie was saying as I drifted off. "Maybe your father's still out there somewhere? Still waiting. What do you think? How would you feel about finding your real dad?"

I nodded, sleepily. A real dad. A real mum. And a lifetime supply of real pies. Like I said—heaven. Pure heaven.